*A Lo*

Lone Pine Five

CW00853769

This Armada book belongs to:

Virginia Allen

Malcolm Saville has been writing Lone Pine stories for over twenty years. Each adventure is complete in itself and there are now nineteen of them. This is the fifth story in the series.

Lone Pine Five

Malcolm Saville

Armada

First published in this (revised) edition in 1972 by
William Collins Sons & Co. Ltd.,
London and Glasgow.
First published in Armada in 1975 by
William Collins Sons & Co. Ltd.,
14 St. James's Place, London SW1A 1PF

Printed in Great Britain by
Love & Malcomson Ltd.,
Brighton Road,
Redhill, Surrey

Contents

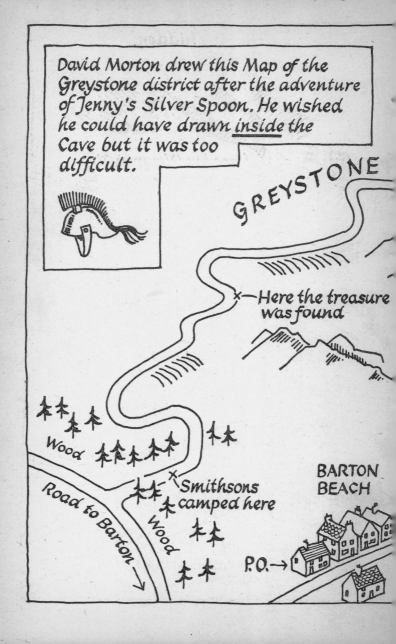

David Morton drew this Map of the Greystone district after the adventure of Jenny's Silver Spoon. He wished he could have drawn <u>inside</u> the Cave but it was too difficult.

GREYSTONE

✕— Here the treasure was found

Wood

Road to Barton →

✕—Smithsons camped here

Wood

BARTON BEACH

P.O. →

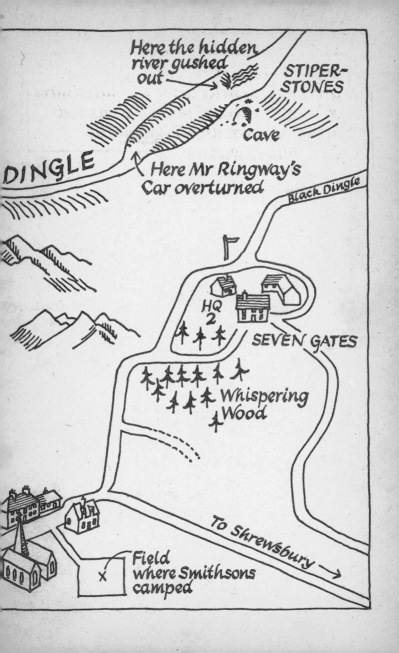

Foreword

Between the Welsh border and a rugged mountain range called the Stiperstones in the County of Shropshire is a tract of wild and desolate country called by some the "Land of Dereliction."

The scene of this story is set in the shadow of the mysterious Stiperstones, which are crowned with black quartzite rocks, older even than the ice-age, known as the Devil's Chair.

Lead was once found in these hills and there is no doubt that the Romans worked the mines because "pigs" of metal, inscribed in Latin "The Lead of the Emperor Hadrian," have actually been found in this area. Although the Stiperstones and the derelict mines do still exist, there is not much other evidence of Roman occupation—no Roman towns, villas, nor even treasure—in that particular little corner of England, but what Mr Wilkins told Jenny about the Mildenhall Treasure is true, and you can go and see it for yourself in the British Museum in London.

There is no place called Barton Beach, no valley named Greystone Dingle, and I must explain now, before you read the story, that, so far as I know, there is no hidden river in those hills. There are parts of the country where such rivers exist—the River Misbourne in the Chiltern Hills, for instance—but such streams usually run through chalk or limestone and the Shropshire hills are made of very different stuff!

I must also explain that this special edition is a little shorter than the original story which was first published in 1949, but the adventure, which I hope you will find exciting, has not been altered. Many readers have asked why it is called *Lone Pine Five*. It is the fifth adventure of the Lone Piners.

M.S.

THE LONE PINE CLUB

THE Lone Pine Club was started by some boys and girls at a lonely farmhouse called Witchend in the highlands of Shropshire. If you have not read any of their other adventures you will probably enjoy this story more if you know something about the Club and its members before you begin.

The rules of the Club, which were originally signed in blood, were very simple and are set out in full in "Mystery at Witchend." The most important was "To be true to each other whatever happens." The headquarters of the Club are at a hidden camp under a lonely pine tree in the Witchend valley, but another meeting-place was established in an old barn at a farm on the Stiperstones known as Seven Gates. This is mentioned in this story and is known as "H.Q.2."

The Lone Piners' secret signal to each other is a whistled imitation of the peewit's haunting call.

The Members

DAVID MORTON. The captain of the Club. In this story he is sixteen. While his father was in the R.A.F. during the war he came with his mother to live at Witchend and has one brother and sister, who are twins. Now the Mortons live in London, but come to Witchend whenever they can.

RICHARD ("DICKIE") MORTON and MARY MORTON are ten, and although they go to separate schools, they are inseparable at all other times. They are alike in looks and speech, and occasionally in thought. They are often extremely irritating to their friends, and particularly to grown-ups, but they have the outstanding qualities of courage and of loyalty to each other.

PETRONELLA ("PETER") STERLING. Peter is sixteen. She has no mother, but lives in the holidays with her father, who is in charge of a reservoir called Hatchholt, not very far from Witchend. She goes to school in Shrewsbury but is only really happy when she is roaming her beloved Shropshire highlands on her Welsh pony, Sally. Imagine Peter with two fair plaits, fearless blue eyes and a clear brown skin. She looks her best in jodhpurs and a blue shirt. She knows the stars better than most of us know a map of the country in which we live. She loves everything in the open air, and can swim faster than most boys of her age and ride better.

She is the Vice-Captain of the Club and David is her boyfriend.

TOM INGLES. Tom is a Londoner who was sent to join his uncle on a farm near Witchend when his home was bombed in the war. He is small for fifteen-and-a-half, but very wiry. It took him a long time to become reconciled to life in the country, but he would not leave farming now. At first he was suspicious of the Mortons and Peter and impatient with the twins, but is now proud of his membership of the Club. He is quick-witted, brave, and liked by everyone who is lucky enough to know him.

JENNY HARMAN. Until now Jenny has not played much part in the Club's adventures. She has a step-mother who is not always very kind to her, and lives at the village shop and post office of a village called Barton Beach on the western side of the Stiperstones. She is red-headed, incurably romantic and two months younger than Tom, who is the staunchest and most wonderful friend she has ever known. This story is really Jenny's.

There are two other members of the Club who do not appear in this book—JONATHAN and PENELOPE ("PENNY") WARRENDER. These two are cousins and firm friends and live in the holidays in a hotel called *The Gay Dolphin* at Rye, in Sussex.

There is one more member of the Morton family, who thinks the Club belongs to him, and he is MACBETH—a black Scottie dog who loves them all, but especially Mary, who has nearly wrecked many an adventure because she will carry Mackie when his short legs tire.

1. The Strange Silver Spoon

ALMOST EVERY MORNING in the summer when she woke and it was light enough to see, Jenny Harman automatically counted the nineteen red roses on the wallpaper between the door and the old wardrobe in the corner.

On the August morning on which this story opens, the sun just reached roses eleven, twelve and thirteen, and made them glow with so rich a colour that the others were really in the shade. Jenny sat up and yawned, as she nearly always did, and wondered what could possibly happen today. Of course she was happy here at home, but she had no brothers or sisters, and Barton Beach was a very small and lonely village and there was not much to do besides help her father sometimes in the shop. Jenny was a romantic and imaginative girl, fond of books and daydreaming. She settled her red head back on the pillows again and her hand reached for the book of the moment. Absorbed, Jenny forgot the time and was late for breakfast.

"Sorry, Mum," she pleaded, when her stepmother greeted her without enthusiasm. "I must have dropped off again."

"Better if you stopped reading, my girl . . . Here's your porridge. Look sharp with it for I've plenty to do today."

Mr Harman looked over the top of his paper at his daughter, and Jenny thought she detected a wink. She smiled at him as she reached for the milk jug. He was an understanding father.

"What to do today, Jen?" he asked. "Looks as if it might keep fine for a bit, so you ought to go out. What's happened to those young friends o' yours over Witchend way?"

"They've not come up yet, Dad. Still at home. I wish they would come."

"And young Tom? Not seen much of him lately?"

Jenny blushed.

"Harvest, Dad. You know how busy Mr Ingles keeps him."

Mr Harman twinkled at the daughter he loved to tease.

"He's got a little time to waste, I'm thinking. Look on the mantelpiece, my lass, and see what the postman has brought you."

Jenny jumped up and knocked her chair over.

"You might have told me, Dad. It's a letter for me. From Tom."

She tore open the envelope.

"DEAR JEN,

Uncle Alf and me coming to market at Bishop's Castle on Tuesday. Maybe you would bike over. Come as soon as you can Uncle says. Meet me at that stall where the chap sells dogs' leads and collars but come early and I've got important news.

Yours,
TOM."

Jenny's eyes shone with happiness.

"Look, Dad. Look, Mum. I can go, can't I? Right away? Come early, he says, and it's Tuesday now!"

"It's a longish ride," Mrs Harman complained, "and I reckon it'll rain soon and there doesn't seem any sense to me in rushing over to the Castle on market day."

But Mrs Harman always put difficulties in the way of such suggestions on principle, and it was not long before Jenny was on her way.

The sun was shining brightly and it was already hot. Jenny knew that it was too bright to last and that it would rain before she was home again, but she was used to cycling in the wet. Now she was so happy that she sang at the top of her voice as she pedalled through the lanes towards the main road which would take her to the market town and to Tom and "Uncle Ingles." If only something like this could happen every day!

The country through which she was riding was bare and forbidding, although she never really thought of it as such, for she was used to it. Before her stretched the purple heather of the moor, with here and there a white and lonely cottage, and behind her the great gaunt ridge of the Stiper-stones range.

Soon she could see the hill which once was crowned by a fortress, and over to her left were the remains of another called Lea Castle. Jenny had often been to see the great boulder in a field near by which was called the Lea Stone, and she knew that this stone was supposed to have been flicked there by the Devil who found it in his shoe when he sat down once to rest on his chair on the summit of the Stiperstones. She knew, too, that the stone was supposed to turn round when the clock strikes thirteen.

Now she was in Bishop's Castle itself, where the traffic was so heavy that she had to jump off her bicycle and walk. The pavements were crowded as well, which made it difficult to hurry, and Jenny was in a hurry, for Tom had said, "Come early."

From the top of the hill Jenny could see the market stalls stretched along the side of the street below her, and she recognized Tom before he saw her. Suddenly she felt shy. It was stupid to be so excited about meeting anyone, however nice he might be.

Then Tom saw her and came to her rescue.

"Hello, Jen," he said, and "Hello, Tom," she answered with flaming cheeks.

"Oh, Tom," she began breathlessly, "isn't this all wonderful? I only got your letter this morning, and I just *forced* Mum to let me come today. What shall we do first, Tom? I don't care how late I am. Where's Mr Ingles, Tom? And you said you'd got some news. What is it?"

"Let's put your bike in the yard of the *Rose and Crown* first and get it out of the way. We've got to meet Uncle there soon for a meal. Then we'll buy an ice and get some-where out of the crowd and have a talk. I've got lots to tell you."

And that was what they did. Each with a large wafer, they climbed the hill again and found a seat against the wall up by the hotel which now stands where the Castle once dominated the little town. The sun was still shining, but big clouds were piling up in the west. Tom sniffed the wind like a true farmer and told Jenny what she knew already.

"Rain's on the way, Jen. Lucky we've got all the harvest in. It's early this year and Uncle says we're lucky. He doesn't often say that, so I reckon we must be . . . If he hadn't said I could come with him today, Jen, I'd have written you a much longer letter—"

Jenny extracted the last delicious fragments of ice-cream from the remains of the sodden wafer, licked her fingers elegantly, and then smiled at him.

"Would you really, Tom? I do wish you would. Nobody ever writes me letters, and I do love them so . . . But why, Tom? What's happened?"

"You'll never let me finish what I'm saying to you, Jenny. Just be quiet and I'll tell you. I've had a letter and it's for you as well. Here it is."

She snatched it from him.

"Beast! Keeping it from me all this time."

She opened the envelope and her heart gave a jump as she saw the Lone Pine symbol at the top of the paper.

"DEAR TOM AND JENNY (she read),

Don't mind this coming to Tom first, Jenny, but I've only time for one letter, and I know Tom will like to send it on to you. How are you both? We know Tom will be busy enough at Ingles, and we expect Jenny is spending her time reading, but you've both got to stop whatever you are doing pretty quickly now, for *we're just about on our way*! In a day or two we'll be at Witchend, and I hope for the rest of the hols. It's been a bit difficult to persuade our parents this year, but we've managed it, and here we come. Father is bringing the car and a trailer full of camping gear, so we'll all be out and about again before very long. Peter has been here for a fortnight, as you know, and is coming back with us and will stay at Witchend while her father is still stopping at Seven Gates. We've had a good time together, but we all want to get back to the good old L.P. Whatever happens, Jenny *must* get permission to come camping with us, and if there's any trouble I'll come over and see Mr Harman—"

"It's *Mrs* Harman he'll have to see," Jenny murmured as she turned the page.

"Anyway," she read on, "you must both be ready for the first meeting of the Club the day after tomorrow, but we'll call in at Ingles on the way up and let you know we've arrived. One other thing, and it's a disappointment. We had hoped to get Jon and Penny to Witchend as well. You'll remember we talked about it at Clun at Christmas, but they can't manage it. They've both gone to Paris to live with a family and improve their French. We've had one or two postcards from Penny already, but I think they'll be back in Rye by the end of the week. Peter sends her love to Jenny, and so do the twins.
                                        See you both soon,
                                                DAVID."

Jenny sighed ecstatically.
"Let me keep this letter, Tom, please . . . I knew this was going to be a wonderful day when your letter came. I forgot to tell you I had a postcard from Penny too. Is it time to meet your uncle now?"

Back at the *Rose and Crown* they found Mr Ingles waiting for them under the archway which led into the big yard behind the inn.

Jenny had never managed to get used to Alfred Ingles,

who was unlike any other farmer she had ever known. She really liked him very much and knew that he was kind-hearted and jolly, but he talked more than most country-men and louder than any.

"Come along in, kids," he roared, "come along in. You've kept me two minutes already . . . How are you, my pretty dear? Pleased to see you, and there was a message for you from the missus, but I've forgotten what it was . . . Not lost your voice, have you, Jenny?"

"No, thank you, Mr Ingles," Jenny gasped, "and I'm fine, thanks, and thank you very much for asking me today. I'm enjoying myself very much," and here she looked up at him so appealingly that he put his hand on her head and ruffled her red hair affectionately.

"And no more *Mister* Ingles, if you please, Jenny lass. Uncle Alf I'm to be to you, same as I am to young Tom here . . . Now then! Here we are."

The dining-room of the *Rose and Crown* was thick with the smell of food, but not many people were talking. They were all too busy eating. Even Mr Ingles quietened as he started lunch, and Tom and Jenny were now enjoying themselves too much to want to talk. While Jenny was waiting for her pudding she noticed an elderly man sitting at a table in the far corner. She glanced at him a second time because he looked out of place and unhappy. He had a thin, studious face, and was wearing horn-rimmed spectacles His forehead was high and he was very bald on the top of his shining head, and he looked like a schoolmaster. Suddenly Jenny felt very sorry for him. Then her pudding arrived and she forgot him.

Mr Ingles pushed back his chair as soon as he had finished eating.

"Now you two can do what you like so long as Tom is back in the car park at half-past three. Not a minute later, mind. 'Bye, Jenny girl. Give your uncle a kiss in case I don't see you again."

Outside, they wondered what would be the best way of spending the afternoon, and then Tom had his big idea.

"They have an auction sale in the yard here every other market day at two o'clock, Jenny. Let's stay and see what happens. Maybe we could buy something—"

When Tom and Jenny went back into the yard they saw a lorry in the far corner unloading second-hand furniture which was being added to the collection of odds and ends already displayed on the cobblestones. A fat man, who was probably the auctioneer, was fussing round and supervising, and three women were picking among the rubbish rather like rooks on a field of stubble. Tom strolled over and Jenny, suddenly filled with the feminine lust of bargain-hunting, followed him.

By the auctioneer's rostrum lay a metal tray filled with odds and ends.

"I wouldn't mind that old knife," Tom said as he turned over the oddments on the tray. "Yes, I would, though— the blade is broken . . . Here's an old pipe, but it smells a bit. I wonder if Uncle would like it."

"I shouldn't think so," Jenny murmured. "Let me look too. What's this? Look, Tom. It's a funny sort of spoon."

Tom glanced at a discoloured object in her hand and then turned away without interest. He was getting bored and wished the performance would begin.

Jenny turned to follow him and then picked up the spoon again. It was certainly a very odd shape. The bowl was pear-shaped and the handle no more than a square-edged strip of metal tapering to a point. It was very dirty—almost black. Suddenly she felt that somehow or other she must possess this spoon, although she had no idea what she could do with it if she had it. It was an odd feeling, and for a moment she felt quite scared, but when Tom turned to see what she was doing, she said:

"I would like this old spoon, Tom. Do you think it would cost much?"

He looked at her and saw that she was serious, so instead of asking a lot of stupid questions about why she wanted it he coloured a little and said:

"All right, Jen. If you really want it I'd like to buy it for you. I wanted to get you something anyway."

"But you can't do that, Tom. Do you mean we'll stay and—and *bid* for it?"

Tom nodded. "Why not?"

"But it might cost *pounds*. And would you do it in front of all these people?"

Tom was beginning to feel flattered.

" 'Course I would. Why not? Let's stay on now and I'll buy it for you, Jen. I'd like to. Honest I would."

Jenny beamed at him and slipped her hand into his arm.

The yard was filling now and soon the auctioneer mounted his stand and started the sale, which was not very exciting, although everyone disputed his suggested price for each particular lot. At last he came to the tray of junk. He seemed to have some difficulty in describing the assortment, but eventually offered it as "this variety of knick-knacks and second-hand cutlery." The crowd laughed at the price suggested but Tom spoke up bravely with an offer for the old spoon. He did not want anything else. When the auctioneer recovered himself and asked the bidder to repeat his offer, Tom reduced it slightly and the dwindling crowd expressed its approval of his bargaining skill! There were no other bidders, so the spoon was passed to Jenny's eager hands. She looked up at Tom with shining eyes and said, "Thank you, Tom. That was wonderful of you, and I'll never forget it—I don't know why I want this so, but I love it already and I'll never part with it. I'm sure it's lucky, Tom, and I think when it's cleaned it will be beautiful too. It's a lovely shape . . . Look!"

And as Tom, a little embarrassed at this show of emotion, but feeling rather pleased with himself just the same, took the little spoon from her fingers, a voice from behind them said:

"Excuse me, my dear, but might I look at that old spoon? Have you just purchased it here—at this sale?"

Jenny grabbed the spoon back from Tom and whirled

round to see who had been looking over her shoulder. She saw a tall, thin man in a suit of grey tweed. He was wearing horn-rimmed spectacles and his tired face for a moment seemed familiar He smiled at her kindly, but vaguely, and then she remembered that he was the man in the corner of the dining-room for whom she had felt sorry.

"All right," she said. "You can look at it if you like. But take care of it. It's precious."

The man took up the dirty little scrap of metal very gently, pushed his spectacles up his forehead and turned to the light so that he could examine it more carefully. Tom stood by fidgeting impatiently and looking at the newcomer with some hostility, but Jenny had again that odd feeling of pity for him.

"May I have it back, please?" she said after a long pause, but the old man did not seem to hear her and was now scraping at the spoon with his thumb-nail and examining it with growing excitement.

"*Please*, sir," Jenny repeated, "may I have my spoon back now? It *is* a spoon, isn't it?"

Then he seemed to notice her, and although he did not at once give her back the spoon, which he was holding very carefully, he put one hand on her shoulder and said in a surprisingly kind and gentle voice:

"Listen to me, little girl. Tell me where you got this— this spoon. Did you pick it up from amongst this rubbish? Is it really yours?"

The yard was empty now but for a man who was stacking the unsold junk together, and the auctioneer who was eyeing the old man and the children curiously.

"Of course it's hers, mister," Tom broke in. "I've just bought it for her. Please give it back at once."

The auctioneer strolled over and spoke to the man in grey.

"Something of value there, sir? I doubt it, but it's true that this lad bought it for a very small sum."

The stranger put a hand to his forehead.

"Incredible!" he gasped. Then, to the auctioneer, "Do

you know where this came from? How came it into your hands?"

The auctioneer stroked his nose reflectively.

"I reckon that lot of rubbish came from an old manor-house over Stiperstones way that was selling up the other day, but if that thing you've got in your hand is valuable it's all the luck of the game, and that lad knows something that some expert has missed. Plenty of people have been through that tray-load before it came here."

The old man stepped over to the tray and carefully examined everything that was left, but found nothing more to interest him. Then he turned to Jenny and said, "There is your spoon my dear, but take it carefully. I would like to look at it again and show it to some friends of mine too, if you wouldn't mind—"

Jenny shook her head violently, grabbed Tom's sleeve, and ran out of the yard with her precious spoon hot in the other hand. But the old man caught them on the pavement. He was very agitated and excited, but in desperate earnest, as he pleaded with them:

"Please, my dear," he said, "please don't run away. I am an old man and I have a great interest in old things, and I think you have something in your hand which is of very great value and interest. I realize that it belongs to you, but I would like to examine it more closely . . . Perhaps you would permit me to take you to some place of refreshment near by and let me look at it again?"

"We've just had our dinner, thanks all the same," Tom said briskly. "And we've got something else to do this afternoon, so we'd better be getting along."

"But wait, *please*, just one minute. Will you give me your name and address, little girl, so that I may come and see the spoon again and examine it, and perhaps talk to your father about it?"

"Talk to Dad about it? Whatever for? And there's another thing, sir. Please don't call me little girl. I know I'm not tremendous, but I'm getting on for sixteen, and my name's Jenny Harman—"

"That's enough, Jenny," Tom broke in again. "No need to tell him about us. Let's get on."

Jenny looked up at the old man to say "Good-bye," and saw the expression on his face. One nervous hand was plucking at his grey moustache and she could see that he was really distressed. Suddenly she was sure that all this really *mattered* to him.

"Just a sec, Tom," she said. "I think this is important . . . What do you really want to know about this old spoon, sir?"

"Jenny," the old man murmured. "That was the name, was it not? Thank you, my dear. Will you and your young friend, who seems to mistrust me, come and sit down somewhere quietly and let me examine that spoon again? It will be quite safe with me, I assure you, and I know that it belongs to you."

Jenny made up her mind. "Come on, Tom."

Tom shrugged his shoulders. He was annoyed and not at all sure that he was not being made to look rather foolish. He had bought the old spoon because Jenny had wanted it, although he considered her to be a little crazy for asking for such a ridiculous thing, and now they had got involved with a foolish old man. But he did have the good sense and the good manners not to start arguing in the street, and when Jenny pinched his arm and whispered, "Sorry, Tom, but I just had to say that, he looked so miserable," he managed a grin.

They went into a little tea-shop called the Brown Owl, where the old man ordered coffee for himself and ice-cream for Tom and Jenny.

"Do not misunderstand me, my dear," the old man said as he held the spoon again, "but I think this is very old. I collect old things and would like to buy this from you. That is why I said I would come and see your father so that he would not think I was being unfair to you . . . I do not believe this is really of much interest to you, but perhaps if I bought it from you—and I most certainly do want it very badly, you would buy something you really want with the

23

money . . . A new bicycle, possibly . . . Would you sell me this old spoon, my dear Jenny?"

Although her best friends sometimes called Jenny scatter-brained, there were occasions when she could be definite. This was one of them. She scooped up the last spoonful of ice-cream, sat back and smiled sweetly at her host.

"What is your name, please?" she asked first.

"Wilkins," he replied.

"Thank you for that ice, then, Mr Wilkins. Now about my spoon. I don't care whether it's worth a million, trillion pounds, or a few pence. I don't care whether it's a million years old or who it belonged to or even where it came from. . . . I just don't care, *but*, Mr Wilkins, I wouldn't sell it for any money in the world."

Mr Wilkins regarded her with respect.

"But why, my dear? It doesn't mean anything to you. It can't do!"

"But it does. I wanted it and Tom gave it to me."

And after this typically feminine argument it was soon obvious that there was nothing more to be said. Mr Wilkins fingered his moustache a little and then gave up trying to persuade her.

"Where do you live, Jenny?" he asked at last. "I would still like to tell your father what I think about the spoon, even if you won't sell it to me . . . I am going to stay up in this country for a while because I am looking round for old things and exploring a little as well."

Tom and Jenny looked at each other meaningly, for it was not so very long ago that they had met another elderly man who was exploring wild and lonely country; he had professed at first an interest in "old things," and later turned out to be someone who was much more interested in the present.* But even although Tom nudged her under the table, Jenny said:

"I live at Barton Beach, and there's a lot of old things round there."

* See *The Secret of Grey Walls*

24

"Barton?" Mr Wilkins said as he produced a map from his pocket. "Barton Beach? Surely that is a village right under the Stiperstones?"

Jenny nodded. "That's right. Have you been there?"

"I was going there, my child. Perhaps you could find me a lodging? I am interested in Barton, for it is reputed to be the best centre from which to explore the old lead mines first opened by the Romans."

"Tom and I know all about those old mines," Jenny replied excitedly. "We had a terrific adventure there not so very long ago . . . If you do come to Barton, Mr Wilkins, I'm sure we can find you somewhere to stay. My Dad keeps the shop and post office and sometimes Mum has a bedroom to let. I'll ask her if you like . . . Now may I have my spoon, please? . . . Thanks!"

Tom glanced at the clock at the back of the shop. So far as he was concerned, it had been a wasted afternoon, although Jenny seemed to have enjoyed herself.

"Sorry," he said, "but we've got to go now, sir. I've got to meet my uncle."

Mr Wilkins was poring over his map, but with great earnestness he begged Jenny to promise that she would take every care of the spoon.

"I really do think, my dear, that you have something valuable there. Take care of it and do not sell it to anybody but me . . . But I shall come and see you at Barton Beach. You can rely upon that. Good-bye!"

Once outside, Tom hurried Jenny along the pavement.

"About this lovely, wonderful spoon, Tom," she said suddenly, "I don't really think I ought to keep it if it really is worth a lot of money. P'raps you ought to have it back?"

They were nearly at the car park now and Tom could see his uncle unlocking the door of the car.

"Have it back, Jenny? Don't be silly. I think old Wilkins is crackers, but that spoon is yours and you stick to it."

"I shall wear it next my heart for always," Jenny said. "Oh, hello, Uncle Alf. Here we are. I've brought him safely back, you see, and if you're really good I'll come and see you the day after tomorrow. The Mortons are coming to Witchend. Did you know?"

Mr Ingles expressed his joy at this news with a mighty roar which drowned the sound of his engine as it started up. Then Tom got in beside him and waved a cheerful "good-bye" as they drove out of the car park.

Jenny waved frantically as Tom leaned from the car window. Then she fingered the spoon in her pocket and walked slowly up the hill to fetch her bicycle just as the first drops of rain fell.

Now the sun had gone from Jenny's day too, and as she pedalled homewards she felt tired and depressed. But she cheered up at the thought of the letter in her pocket and that the day after tomorrow the Mortons and Peter would be back. Then she thought of old Mr Wilkins and his interest in the strange little silver spoon, and wondered whether it really was valuable. She still did not know quite why she had said she wanted it, although it was unusual. She had told Tom that she would wear it next her heart always, which was stupid of her, because it was an awkward shape and would be uncomfortable, but as she fingered it she noticed that the tapering handle was fixed to the bowl by a little loop or scroll of metal.

"I could thread some ribbon through that and wear it round my neck," she thought, "but it wouldn't do to let anyone know. They'd think it was silly."

It was now raining very hard. Soon Jenny felt the wet against her shoulders and knew that her raincoat was sodden.

A mile farther on she caught up a friend of her step-mother's just as she was going into her cottage gate. Jenny did not much care for Mrs Greenside, and she liked her still less for asking her to wait in the porch while she searched for a magazine which she wished Mrs Harman to see. She kept poor Jenny waiting for nearly a quarter of an hour, and by the time she pushed her bicycle into the shed behind the shop the magazine was wetter than Jenny herself. Feeling thoroughly cold and miserable, she let herself in, rather hoping that her stepmother would be upstairs. But she was not. She was in the kitchen making tea.

"Out of those clothes, my girl, and into a hot bath this instant . . . Wait there and I'll fetch you a towel and a dressing-gown, for you can't go upstairs dripping water all over the house."

Five minutes later Jenny was wrapped in her dressing gown and sipping scalding tea in front of the kitchen fire.

"That will soon warm you through, lass," Mrs Harman said. "Maybe you'll come to no harm, but I told you how it would be . . . You're a wilful girl." But she smiled as she said this and Jenny knew that she was not really cross. Rather did she seem to have something on her mind, and after a moment's pause she went on:

"He's come, Jenny. Where did you meet him?"

"Who's come, Mum? What do you mean?"

"Not more than fifteen minutes ago this man called. Tall and thin and elderly, he is. He came on a bike and said he'd met you at Bishop's Castle and you'd told him I might have a room for him."

Jenny giggled. "Oh, Mum! I never thought he would come. Tom and I met him after dinner . . . I s'pose he must have passed me while I was waiting at Mrs Greenside's . . . Do you mind, Mum? I didn't really think much about it, but he said he wanted to stay in Barton . . . I think he's all right. I liked him, but Tom bought me an old spoon at the *Rose and Crown* sale, and this Mr Wilkins says it's worth a lot of money."

"He spoke well and friendly of you, Jen, so, as we might as well have someone who will pay for it in the spare room, I've told him he can stay. He's in the bath now, so you must wait till he's finished."

Jenny laughed and reached for a biscuit. "I'm warm now, thanks, Mum, but I'll wait a bit and have a bath when he's out of the way . . . Can I ask you something special, please? . . . Well, it's not much really. May I have a boiled egg for my supper?"

"You can have two if you like. Why?"

" 'Cos I've got a special spoon to eat eggs with," she said triumphantly, before the expression on her face changed and she cried, "I *did* have one, anyway . . . What did you do with my raincoat, Mum? I left it in the pocket," and with that she dashed into the kitchen.

2. *Witchend Again*

T WO DAYS LATER, at half-past ten on another sunny morning, Tom closed the gate of Ingles Farm carefully behind him and began his summer holiday. As he turned to the right up the stony lane that he knew so well, he took again from the pocket of his corduroy trousers the two cards which had come by the morning post. The first was from David Morton: "Should arrive about eleven-thirty," and the other was from Jenny. The message on the latter was much longer and rather more involved, and Tom smiled as he read for the third time:

"Cannot understand why I have not heard when they are coming why don't people tell me Tom just because I have to live out of the world at Barton. Whatever happens I shall come over tomorrow by the bus so meet me Tom without fail at Onnybrook about eleven. Mr W. is still here and most mysterious I am sure and I am now wearing my lovely spoon.

JENNY."

"If they arrive about the same time, Jen will say it's an act of Fate," he laughed. "And I wonder what she means about wearing her spoon?"

At the top of the hill, where the Witchend lane joined the road, Tom stopped for a minute. Although he did not often think about it he nearly always paused here and glanced back across his uncle's fields to the rolling grandeur of the Long Mynd mountain, which stretched across the horizon for twelve miles from nearly north to south. The Mynd, unlike the Stiperstones not so very far away towards Wales, was smooth and rolling—a long plateau of wild moorland

29

with steep valleys, or "gutters" as they were called locally, on the eastern side. One of these valleys was called Hatch-holt, where Peter's father lived by the reservoir. It will be fun to see Peter and the others again, Tom thought. Then he turned and strode down the hill towards the village of Onnybrook, whistling musically as he went.

A mile and a half farther on the road crossed a clear, rushing stream, then twisted sharply to the left under an arch of overhanging trees and met the railway at a level-crossing, the gates of which were closed. A bell rang sharply in the signal-box and the signalman, who waved cheerily to Tom, strained at a lever as a train roared through on its way to Ludlow, Hereford and the south. When it had passed, Tom saw Jenny waiting on the other side of the gates. They both said "Hello" at the same time, but Jenny added: "You might have been here, Tom, like I asked you. When I got off the bus you just weren't there, and I wondered if you'd had my postcard. Did you?"

"Of course I did, but I couldn't read it properly. Half a sec, Jen. Old George is opening the gates. Stay where you are. I'm coming over."

"I've got a lot to tell you, Tom," Jenny said as the gates began to open, "but tell me first if you've got any news. When are they coming?"

"Any minute now," Tom said. "They'll come Ludlow way, I reckon, so let's watch for them," and almost before he had finished speaking Jenny pointed to a large grey car rounding the corner a hundred yards away.

"It's them!" Jenny shouted, and ran into the middle of the road waving wildly. "Look, Tom! And they're towing a trailer."

The car pulled into the side of the road and Peter and David were out almost before it had stopped. There was such a noise that Mrs Morton put her hands over her ears and her husband pressed his horn to restore order. The startled hush that followed was broken by the sharp bark of a Scottie terrier from somewhere in the rear, and then:

"Good morning, Tom and Jenny." It was Dickie's voice,

and as Tom went over Mary broke in and once again he was astonished that any brother and sister could be so alike. Apart from looks, where, of course, Mary's longer hair gave her away, their voices, manner of speaking, and even choice of words seemed interchangeable and more alike than ever.

"Help us out, please, Tom," she said. "Mackie first, of course. He wants to stretch his legs. You've no idea how good he's been on this terrible journey. Do you know we started in the night—acksherly in the night and had breakfast on the way? . . . Thank you, Tom . . . Hello, Jenny. Isn't this an exciting, wonderful meeting?"

After a few minutes Tom and Jenny then squeezed into the back of the car with David and Peter, but the twins said they would walk up the hill with Macbeth. There was some argument following this decision because Mrs Morton did not seem to trust them ever to reach Witchend, but David assured his mother that the idea behind the suggestion to walk was simple enough—they did not wish to help with the unpacking and getting straight.

Dickie regarded his brother coldly.

"P'raps you and Peter would like to walk," he said. "Mary and me know you're a thought-reader, o' course—"

"If he has any thoughts ever," Mary interrupted.

"—but we'd like you to have a quiet think some time about minding your own business. We don't expect Mother will mind if we walk and call in and see Mr and Mrs Ingles on the way."

And so it was agreed without further argument.

The advance party in the car called in first at Ingles, where a great welcome awaited them, and although Mrs Ingles begged them all to stay to dinner to save trouble, it was at last arranged that Tom and Jenny, together with the twins when they arrived, should stay at the farm for a meal and go on to Witchend later.

So Mr and Mrs Morton, with David and Peter, drove on to Witchend. It was just the same. Nothing changed. There was the larch wood clinging to the side of the steep valley.

There was the house itself, with its two gabled windows under the roof, leaning against the hillside. There was the white gate between the low stone walls just where the lane stopped, and there was the same stream of clear, cold water gushing under the wall and singing down the side of the lane towards Ingles.

Mr Morton got out of the car and sniffed.

"It's good to be back . . . Smells nice and clean! . . . Look! There's Agnes at the door."

Agnes Braid was housekeeper and friend to them all. She lived not very far away, and whenever the Mortons visited Witchend she came up to look after them. After David and his father had uncoupled the trailer and put the car away in the old barn, Agnes was still in the porch welcoming the others.

"And where are those precious scamps of mine?" she was saying.

"Mrs Morton got tired of them and threw them away," Peter laughed, "but we're afraid they'll turn up later."

"But when they do arrive just remember that they've had dinner at Ingles," Mrs Morton added, "and do please try not to spoil them so much this time, Agnes."

Two and a half hours later David and Peter came out of the white gate and turned to the right up the valley by the side of the stream. David was carrying a kettle and a bucket, and Peter a rucksack. The sun was hot and the flies hummed over the bracken, but up to their left the larches whispered softly in a breeze which could not be felt down in the valley.

"What time did you tell them, David?" Peter asked.

"I told Tom about a quarter-past three. He'll be on time and see that the others are there too, but I thought it wouldn't be a bad idea if we got up there first . . . It's good to be back, Peter. You never get tired of this place, do you?"

"I told you so only an hour or so ago, didn't I?"

"Quite right," David agreed. "Remember the day we found this place?"

"*We?*" Peter was indignant. "You had nothing to do with it. You were lazing about in the stream here with Dickie when Mary found it . . . And I was with Mary, don't forget."

But she was not really annoyed. She remembered that wonderful day only too well and how it had been the beginning of the Lone Pine Club and all their adventures together.

"Well, let's have another look at it now, anyway," David went on. "Wait a sec, while I fill the kettle and bucket."

They crossed the stream and toiled up the hill at the edge of the wood where the bracken was breast-high and all the time they could see the great lonely pine tree still standing sentinel above them.

"Bring some sticks and kindling if you can manage them," David gasped. "I can't look after anything except this bucket."

Then they turned to the right at the top of the hill, struggled on through gorse and bracken for another hundred yards, and then walked down the hill again a few steps into the smooth, grassy plateau which was their secret camp. On three sides the retreat was walled in by gorse, and it seemed to them both that this was higher and more impenetrable than ever this year. There stood the great tree in serene and lonely majesty, and there were the three flat stones which made their fireplace.

Peter dropped the rucksack and flung herself down on the turf. She lay on her back and through half-closed eyes looked up at the sky between the branches of the pine. David squatted beside her and for a long time neither of them spoke.

Eventually, "You know Father said we could all camp out somewhere if the weather holds, don't you?" David said. "I mean for some days—not just in the garden . . . Shall we try it here? We've never camped at night here."

"Difficult to bring all the gear up without the trailer, though, of course, we can manage it in time . . . Let's wait and see what happens when we've all discussed it together. I've got a hunch something is going to happen to us all, David, and you know I'm generally right."

"Sometimes you're hopelessly wrong," David replied, "but you never remind me of those times! . . . I don't really think there would be room for three tents up here. We wouldn't have space to turn round . . . Listen, Peter. Can you hear what I hear?"

Peter sat up and laughed. "Of course I can. It's Tom, but he's so good at mimicking a peewit that I can't tell the difference now."

Clear and sweet from the wood came the secret call of the Lone Piners—"Peewit . . . peewit!" and Peter pulled herself by a dangling rope into the tree which they used as a lookout and answered Tom's call.

"I can see them, David. They're just coming out of the wood—Tom, Jenny, the twins, and Mackie too."

"They're making too much noise," David answered. "Anybody might be about, and we don't want this place discovered now that we've kept it secret for so long . . . Come down and help me with the fire, Peter."

And while they blew the glowing twigs into flame and balanced the kettle on its three flat stones over the fire, they heard the others crashing through the undergrowth, and then Mackie, with an excited bark, dashed into the little clearing and jumped over David in his excitement.

"Oh, David," Jenny said as soon as she stood under the tree again, "this is wonderful. I've been *longing* for this day —just living for it . . . And I've got such a lot to tell you all. Shall I start now? I mean—before we have tea or anything?"

Peter ruffled her hair.

"Glad you're still alive, anyway, Jen, but if David agrees we'd better sign the book first and then you can tell us everything presently."

The twins sat back on their heels and watched their brother critically as, with his knife, he prised up a square of turf between the roots of the tree and brought to light

34

the old sardine tin which held the rules of the Lone Pine Club and the signatures of all the members written in their own blood. At the bottom of the tin was a little notebook, and in this they all signed their names under the date which David wrote at the top of the page.

"I wish Jon and Penny were here," Peter said. "Once I used to think this Club was big enough without anybody else after Jenny, but I know I was wrong."

Dickie, who had been looking round suspiciously, said suddenly, "Have you two brought any food? I see there's a pail of water so that you can do the washing-up without carrying the dishes down to the stream—"

"Like you usually force us to do," Mary added brightly.

"—but where's the tea?" Dickie went on. "You've had all this time to get something arranged, and it doesn't look as if you've done much. *We* had to walk all the way, and if it hadn't been for Mr and Mrs Ingles we'd never have got here at all. We'd have been starved. Utterly famished."

When Mary was silly enough to say that what they all needed was "action and not words," Tom and Jenny fell on the twins until they were forced to plead for mercy. Then Peter made the tea, and while they were drinking it Jenny said, "Now can Tom and me tell our story?"

"It's Jen's story really," Tom said quickly. "I didn't have much to do with it."

"You had *everything* to do with it, Tom! If you hadn't bought me the spoon—"

"And then I s'pose you bought Tom a fork!" Mary said cheekily as she rolled Macbeth on to his back and tickled his tummy, but at last they persuaded Jenny to start at the beginning and tell them about her treasure.

Once she got really started nothing could stop her, and her description of the auction sale in the yard of the inn at Bishop's Castle was so dramatic that her hearers could almost imagine a mob of excited buyers bidding frantically against each other until Tom stepped in calmly and bought the spoon just because Jenny wanted it.

"It must have cost an awful lot of money," Mary said

pensively. "I think it was wonderful of Tom to get it for you like that."

Jenny looked at her gratefully. "It was," she said, and fortunately did not see Tom wink at David.

"What I want to know before we go any further," Dickie interrupted loudly, "is what on earth Jenny wanted a spoon for. It's such a silly thing to make a fuss about . . . And when is something going to happen in this story, anyway?"

Jenny turned her back on him and addressed herself to Peter and David, who, although they did not show it, were also wondering when she was coming to the point. But she came to Mr Wilkins at last and was rewarded when the twins stopped fidgeting and sat up to listen.

"Thin and grey he is," Jenny said dramatically. "Thin and grey and weary-looking. And he says the spoon is very valuable and he wants to talk to Dad about it and buy it from me. Of course, I shall never sell it 'cos Tom bought it for me. Would you all like to see it?" And suddenly she fiddled at her neck and pulled out the spoon on a ribbon.

They crowded round and examined it politely, but it was difficult to imagine that it was of any value, and Peter murmured, "It's not very comfortable to wear, is it, Jen?"

"Oh, I don't mind that a bit," Jenny replied. "I don't mind being a bit uncomfortable, honestly I don't . . . Now listen again, 'cos I haven't finished this story yet . . . Mr Wilkins is this poor old man's name, but in my mind and in my heart I call him the thin, grey man. And now I think you'll all agree that I'm some use to this Club, 'cos if what he says is true then it might be an adventure for us, and he's nice and handy as well, 'cos he's living in our house at the post office."

"But what's he there for, Jenny?" David laughed. "You haven't told us that yet."

"It's easy," Dickie said before Jenny could answer. "It's the easiest thing I ever heard. I bet he's a detective like Mr Cantor at Clun. It's funny how we get mixed up with crime."

"But he's not a bit like that, Dickie," Jenny explained. "He's kind and gentle and quite old, and I'm sure he wants helping. And he's so *nice*," she continued. "Really and truly he is. He's not a bit like a criminal or even a detective . . . He's not like anyone I've ever met or read about. I do wish you'd all believe me . . ."

"I believe you think so, Jenny," said David. "But tell us what else has happened to make you so excited."

"Oh, dear," she said. "Haven't I told you that yet? My nice Mr Wilkins says that this old spoon that Tom bought for me was made by the Romans when they lived round here. He says it's Roman treasure and that he's come specially to the Stiperstones and to Barton to find out more things about the Romans who dug lead out of the mines round home, and he says do I know anyone who really knows the country and will help him search."

David stopped whittling at the stick he was holding between his knees, the twins stopped playing with Macbeth, Tom sat up straight, and Peter put her hands behind her head, lay back in the sunshine and looked up pensively between the branches of the Lone Pine at the sky, which was as blue as her eyes.

"I hope you told him that you knew the very people, Jenny, darling . . . Did you think of all your little Lone Pine friends?"

But even before Jenny could answer, Mary and Dickie stood up.

"When do we start? I s'pose we could go tonight, couldn't we?"

"The best thing about this Club is that everyone does something for it," Dickie added with remarkable common-sense. "See what Jenny has done for us now. She's found us another adventure."

"I s'pose he won't run away before we get there, will he, Jen?" was Tom's awful thought, and "How can we all get there and help him?" came from Peter. "Do you know anything about Roman history, David? Does it make sense to you?"

37

David rubbed his nose reflectively.

"This is where we want Jon. He'd know right away, but I'm sure there's something in it. I know I read somewhere about the Romans mining lead in Shropshire, but anyway, Jenny lives round there. You believe it's possible, don't you, Jen?"

"Of course I do, David. I'm sure my spoon is real, and I know Dad has often told me stories about the Romans, and I do want you all to know how glad I am that I've found Mr Wilkins for the Club. I'd be jolly proud to think I'd found an adventure for the Lone Piners."

Peter jumped to her feet.

"You are silly, Jenny. The Club wouldn't mean a thing without you. Maybe this is going to be your own special adventure. You've certainly found your man! Now let's make some plans. What can we do, David? I don't like the look of the weather, by the way. The sun's gone in and yet the sky looks clear. It'll rain soon."

David took over.

"We've already got permission to go camping," he began, "and we've brought all the gear with us in the trailer. If Jenny's thin grey man means business, then we could perhaps camp somewhere near Barton and do anything we can in the daytime to help him explore. If there's heavy digging to be done we can always put the twins and Mackie on to that. But the great thing is obviously for Jenny to tell the old chap that we really will come and help him, and that he can rely on us."

"Even if he turns out to be a flop," Peter said, "we can have plenty of fun camping in that country on our own. After all, we do know something about it, and didn't we say we'd go back to Black Dingle one day? And we could go to Seven Gates, I suppose. Daddy's there for a few days now with Uncle Micah and Aunt Carol."

"Of course we could," Mary added. "I'm sure they'd be pleased to see us. And, o' course, my wonderful Charles is there now."

"Never mind Charles," Dickie said, "but I suppose we

38

could use the barn with the white doors as H.Q.2 again if it's wet. Let's go tomorrow, David."

"How are we going to get the trailer over to Barton? We can't haul it over two mountains."

"I know," said Dickie, "let's ask Dad to tow it over by car and then you big strong ones can pull it the rest of the way."

"That is a good idea, Dickie," his brother said. "Except the last part, of course. I think Father would do that for us . . . Now what about Jenny? Are you going home tonight, Jen?"

"Oh, yes, David. I've got to do that. I'm going on the bus presently, but I needn't go till the last one—unless you think I ought to go earlier and guard dear old Mr Wilkins."

Peter laughed. "Don't you dare let him escape, Jenny. He's your idea. You found him and you mustn't lose him. Guard him well for us . . . What about Tom? Can you come with us tomorrow?"

Tom explained that he was now on holiday, and then they tidied the camp, stamped out the ashes of the fire, and went down the hill again to Witchend.

It was a dull, grey evening when they reached the old house. There was an affecting meeting between Agnes and the twins and then they told Mr Morton of their plan to camp over by the Stiperstones, but not about the thin grey man, and he agreed to take them all and the trailer over to Barton Beach the next morning.

Then Jenny said she must go down to Onnybrook to catch her bus, so David, Peter and Tom walked down to the village with her. It was nearly dusk when the familiar red bus arrived, and as she jumped aboard and waved to them all standing by the side of the road, Jenny was sure she had never been so happy.

3. Black Dingle

JENNY LEANED BACK in her seat and half closed her eyes as the bus meandered through narrow lanes in the summer dusk. She was very happy. It was nice to feel pleasantly tired at the end of a lovely day, and as soon as she was home she must make an excuse for going to see Mr Wilkins and tell him that the Lone Piners were coming tomorrow to help him search for Roman treasure.

"Here you are, young Jenny! Wake up, lass! Looks to me as if your dad has come along to meet you," came the conductor's voice. She scrambled out and was waving to the conductor when she felt a familiar hand on her shoulder and a well-loved voice said, "Hello, Jen. Had a good day?"

"Yes, thank you, Dad, it's been a *marvellous* day. The Mortons have come to Witchend again and Peter is staying with them too, and Tom's got a holiday. They've brought tents and sleeping-bags, and tomorrow Mr Morton is bringing all the camping things over in a trailer behind the car and we're going to camp out somewhere near. I can go with them, can't I, Dad?"

There was a pause while Mr Harman lit his pipe.

"Don't see why not, Jen. I like you to be with your friends."

"Oh, *thank you*. I've never had such a happy holiday as this is going to be . . . It was nice of you to come to the bus and meet me, Dad. Did you come specially?"

"Yes, Jen, I did. I reckoned you'd be on this one, and I just wanted to stretch my legs. I hope you'll get your camp, but there's rain on the way."

"How's Mr Wilkins, Dad? Is he all right?"

Her father looked down at her sharply.

"Why? Why do you ask like that, child? You sound very interested."

"Not particularly. I think he's rather sweet, and after all, I found him for us."

Mr Harman led his daughter over to a field gate they were passing.

"Sit here for a bit with me, Jenny," he said. "I want to have a word with you about Mr Wilkins."

With a little shiver of apprehension Jenny climbed to the top bar of the gate and put her hand on her father's shoulder as he leaned back and puffed at his pipe.

"Why, Dad? What's wrong? What's happened to him?"

"Nothing has happened to him, Jen, but something rather odd has happened to do with him, and I reckoned I'd tell you about it because you might know what it all means, for I don't."

"Tell me, Dad. Quickly."

"It's like this, then, Jen. 'Bout an hour or more ago the telephone in the shop rings and when I answers it a man's voice says was I the postmaster, and when I says 'yes,' he says he is sorry to trouble me but he thought I might know if an old gentleman called Wilkins was staying in Barton. You can be sure this took my breath away, and I was just going to ask why he asked me when he said he was sure the post office would know as soon as anybody else in a village when a stranger arrived. This seemed reasonable enough, so I told the chap that old Wilkins was staying with us, and then I heard him give a sort of whistle and ask if he could speak to him."

Jenny shifted uncomfortably on the bar of the gate.

"Go *on*. What happened?"

"Nothing much. I mean not enough. I went up to Mr Wilkins's room and found him studying maps spread out on the table. When I told him he was wanted on the phone he looked up and said very sharp like, 'Who wants me, Mr Harman? I don't want to speak to anyone. I refuse to speak on the telephone. I don't want anyone to know I'm here. I want to be left alone and in peace, and that is why I've come here.' And while he was saying this, Jen, he was shaking all over and looked pretty scared, and I had to tell him that I'd already told the caller that he was living with us. When I said this I thought he was going to be ill. 'Ask the name, Mr Harman. If it's Smithson I'll have nothing to do with him. Nothing at all. I don't mind what you say, but I'll have nothing to do with it. I won't speak. I don't want them to know where I am. Please go away now.'

"After that there was nothing I could do but go back to the telephone. The man was still there, and when I asked his name he said it was Smithson, and I had to make up some yarn about old Wilkins being out . . . Tell the truth, Jen, I didn't care for the fellow at the other end—nasty, cocksure type. He said Mr Wilkins was his uncle and implied that the old chap wasn't quite right in his head."

"What a *vile* thing to say! I'm sure he's all right, aren't you?"

Mr Harman puffed at his pipe before he answered.

"I suppose so, Jenny. But he is a bit odd, I reckon. That's what I wanted to ask you about. Tell me again everything that happened at the Castle and how he came up to you and what he said."

So Jenny went over the whole story for the second time that day and her father listened carefully.

"And so I'm sure he's just a kind and gentle old man and that there's nothing wrong with him at all," she finished. "What else did that horrible Smithson say?"

"He said Wilkins was a widower and lived with them so that he could be properly looked after. Far as I could make out, this Smithson implied that the old chap had gone off on his own on some crazy expedition and that they were coming over to fetch him home . . . I don't like it much, Jenny, but I don't see what we can do about it. I told Mum, but she said that as long as Mr Wilkins likes to stay with us and pay he could do so. That's all very well, but she didn't hear that oily Smithson on the telephone . . . We don't want any trouble, do we, Jen?"

Jenny slipped off the gate and slid her hand into his.

"We've got to protect Mr Wilkins from his deadly enemies, Dad. That's what we've got to do, but he needn't worry 'cos the others are coming tomorrow, and we'll take care of him. But you must help me tonight, Dad. I must keep him safe for the others . . . Let's go in now. I'm hungry."

Jenny's supper was waiting for her, but while she was eating it she was worrying about Mr Wilkins and wondering what excuse she could make to slip up to his room. At last she gave up the struggle, and before she had finished eating turned to her stepmother and said:

"This is lovely cocoa, Mum. Wouldn't Mr Wilkins like a cup? Shall I take one up to him?"

"He'd be stupid if he didn't like it, my lass, but he'll have no chance to taste it tonight, for I shan't make any more."

"But I'll take some up now if you like. I want to ask him something," Jenny pleaded.

"You'll be clever if you find him, then, for I can't. I've been up twice, but I reckon he's gone out, though I didn't hear him go."

Jenny caught her breath sharply, but when she glanced at her father he put his finger to his lips as if he did not want her to say any more just then. Almost automatically Jenny collected the supper things on to a tray and it was while she was washing them up that she had her idea. Although she could hardly stop yawning, and it was now nearly ten o'clock, she fetched her raincoat and put her head round the sitting-room door.

"I've washed up, Mum. Just going out for a bit. I think I know where Mr Wilkins has gone. Shan't be long," and she slammed the door and ran out into the street.

It was dark now but for the moon. Heavy clouds were piling up from the west and over the little village street loomed the great ridge of the Stiperstones. Jenny was not certain where Mr Wilkins had gone, but she was determined to find him if she could, and she did remember telling him about Black Dingle—one of the steep valleys which led up to the Devil's Chair.

She ran on up the hill until the lights of the village were out of sight. She passed the first lane on the right and took the second. All was very quiet and the trees seemed to close in round her as she went on stubbornly. Somehow she felt that if Mr Wilkins was wandering about by himself he would be likely to make for the dingle.

After a little she turned sharp to the left on a rough track leading uphill through the heart of a wood. As she walked she whistled to keep up her courage. The moon came out from behind the clouds as she left the trees behind her and saw, two hundred yards ahead, the gaunt shape of the old signpost that pointed the way up the dingle to the Devil's Chair.

Then she nearly screamed, for in the light of the fitful moon she thought she saw a strange, shadowy figure that might be that of a man, slumped against the foot of the signpost. Every instinct and fear of the unknown urged Jenny to turn and run as she had never run before down the hill, through the whispering wood, into the lane and down the road to home. She stopped and turned, and then, in fearful fascination, looked back over her shoulder. The strange shape moved and she cried out as she saw that it was a man—or the ghost of a man—that waved thin arms towards her.

Thin arms! He was very tall and thin, and perhaps after all it was Mr Wilkins.

Jenny stood still, but poised for instant flight. The shape seemed to be peering towards her, and after a little a thin voice called "Who is there? Who called?" and then she knew that her instinct had been right and that this was the man whom she had come out to find.

"It's all right, Mr Wilkins," she called. "It's Jenny Harman, your friend. I came to find you."

They turned towards each other at the same time, and when they met, the old man said:

"Indeed you are my friend, child, to have come out tonight to find me . . . Perhaps you are the only friend I have . . . Why are you here? Have they come for me so soon?"

"Nobody has come for you so far as I know, Mr Wilkins, and I've run nearly all the way from home. I heard you'd gone out, and somehow I guessed you might come to Black Dingle, so I thought I'd see if I could find you and tell you some wonderful news."

He did not move.

"Jenny?" he said quietly. "A pretty name for a pretty child. Tell me, Jenny, what is your wonderful news?"

"I don't think I can tell you standing still in this place, Mr Wilkins. I wish you'd take me home because, to tell you the truth, I've always hated this dingle, and most particularly at night, and I'm very frightened of the wood too."

He looked down and smiled at her strangely.

"Come, then, child. You must show me the way, for I have forgotten how I came, and we will both forget our fears. First, tell me your wonderful news, Jenny."

"Listen, Mr Wilkins. You remember you asked me if I knew anyone who knew the country round here well and would help you search for all the Roman things you want to find? . . . Well, I've found six people—or five others besides me—and if you'll have us we'll help you search every day for the rest of the holidays . . . At least I think I can promise that, although I haven't asked the others. You see, I know all the country round here specially, 'cos I was born here and I've never lived anywhere else. And then there's Peter too."

Now that she had started she found it rather difficult to explain the Lone Pine Club to him. Although he was certainly polite and did not once laugh at her, she could not help feeling that he was not taking her seriously.

"Now listen, Mr Wilkins," she said angrily. "You're not being fair. Dad told me about the telephone call that came for you, and although that isn't really our business we would like you to know that the six of us really will help you search. We're bringing tents and camping things tomorrow. We're not kids, Mr Wilkins, and we've had lots of adventures already. You can trust us, Mr Wilkins, but if you want to search these dingles and look round the old lead mines and that sort of thing, we'll help you. Do believe me, please."

Mr Wilkins patted her on the shoulder and she wriggled away.

"No. You needn't believe me now. Just wait till you see the others. They're coming tomorrow, and then you'll see for yourself what we're like and we'll tell you some of the things we could do to help you . . . Just for a change, Mr Wilkins, will you tell me something about these Roman things and what you want to find and whether you've got to dig and what happens if you, or anyone else, finds some treasure in a hole?"

This was very astute of her because, although her companion was not at all used to children—or not to nice children, as we shall see presently—he did really like Jenny for her kindness and friendliness. She also had something which he coveted very badly, and when she had forgotten this nonsense about a pack of children and showed an intelligent curiosity in the subject which was his life's greatest interest, he talked to her easily enough as they walked down towards the main road.

He told her about a Britain which was once largely covered by dense forests, through which wild beasts roamed —a Britain to which the proud Romans came in great galleys rowed by slaves. He told her how some of the Romans later became converts to Christianity, and how he believed Jenny's spoon to be a Christening Spoon which had survived some sixteen centuries.

"Your spoon, my dear," he said, "is much like those Christening Spoons which formed part of the Mildenhall treasure. It is possible that it has a monogram engraved upon its bowl, which consists of the Greek letters 'Kh' and 'R' which in turn are the initial letters of the name of Christ. Perhaps you will permit me to examine the spoon again when we get home—or tomorrow morning."

"Tell me about this Mildenhall place that I've never heard of," Jenny broke in. "We'll look at the spoon tomorrow if you like—before the others come."

They walked on down to the lane while he told her of the grandest discovery of Roman silver of modern times. He told her how in the years A.D. 365–367 a series of terrible disasters overwhelmed many of the defences of the Roman Province in Britain, and of how many Romans buried their silver and valuables so that they should not be discovered by the looting and avenging Picts, Scots and Saxons. He went on to tell her of the farmer and his ploughman who were at work on a field close to the fen in East Anglia during the winter of 1942–43, when the ploughshare, which had been set a little deeper than usual, ran against an obstruction and fell off. The ploughman jumped down to see what had caused the check and found what appeared to be a metal dish. When this was moved it was seen that the dish had been placed upside-down and covered many other articles made of a similar metal, which the two men believed to be pewter or lead. When they finished digging they had unearthed thirty-four lovely pieces, including trays, dishes, goblets, finger-bowls and spoons.

"I have been to see this hoard of treasure in the British Museum many times, my child, and I am sure that the spoon you picked up by chance is similar to those now famous Christening Spoons found at Mildenhall. One day, if you will permit me, we will take your spoon to someone whose knowledge is greater than mine. What you have, my dear, cannot be valued in money, but I believe it was found in these hills and that if we could find the remains of a Roman villa hereabouts, as they did at Mildenhall, then we may well find treasure which those who lived in the villa may have hidden for safety's sake. The Romans mined lead in these hills, Jenny. There was a Roman city not many miles away, at the place we now call Wroxeter—it was called Viroconium then—and there must be Roman villas hereabouts, and I mean to find them."

His voice had a confident ring now as he strode along.

"Of course I understand, Mr Wilkins," Jenny said. "It all sounds wonderful, and I know we can help you . . . We'll come and see you tomorrow as soon as the others

47

arrive and make some plans. You won't go searching by yourself first, will you?"

"Eh?" He stopped and turned round so suddenly that she bumped into him. "Not search by myself? But I *want* to be by myself. That's why I left the others so that I could explore myself, and now it seems that I was stupid enough to talk too freely before them, for they are coming after me and I know they will make me miserable again and interfere with my plans."

He was talking half to himself now, and Jenny realized that her father's guess was apparently correct. She was not quite sure whether to keep quiet in the hope that he would say more, or to question him so naturally that he might answer her without remembering who she was. She decided on a question.

"What happens to anything that you do find, Mr Wilkins? I mean, is it yours right away just because you found it, and could you sell it?"

"Sell it!" he shouted. "It is treasure trove, my child."

"But I don't know what treasure trove is. Please explain. . . . Oh, Mr Wilkins, we're nearly home now. May I bring you some cocoa to your room and will you tell me then before I go to bed?"

He smiled at her gently.

"But you should have been in bed hours ago, child. Are you not too tired?"

"I shan't sleep till I know," Jenny said as she stifled another yawn.

Then they saw Mr Harman hurrying towards them, and when they met Jenny said: "It's quite all right, Dad. I met Mr Wilkins on his way home, and he's been telling me some wonderful things."

The old man put his hand on Jenny's shoulder. "Thank you for letting her come, Mr Harman. I was very glad to see her, and she has proved an admirable guide. I hope your wife will not object, but I have asked your daughter to share a little refreshment with me in my sitting-room. I know it is late, but a few more minutes will not make much difference now. I trust you will permit her to come?"

And, rather to her astonishment, Jenny found herself ten minutes later in pyjamas and dressing-gown sitting on the edge of a big chair in Mr Wilkins's room with a mug of hot cocoa warming her hands.

"This is fun," she said. "Tell me about treasure trove."

"Well," said Mr Wilkins, "objects of gold or silver which have been secretly hidden—not just lost—in soil or in buildings, and of which the original owner cannot be traced, are treasure trove and the property of the Crown."

Jenny understood what this meant, but asked, "Who decides whether it was secretly hidden and what happens when it belongs to the country?"

Then, very patiently, he explained that the local coroner decided whether the discovery was treasure trove or not, and that if it was the Crown would usually pass it over to a museum.

"That sounds dull," Jenny interrupted. "I'm not very keen on scratching about these valleys just because we may find something which will be handed to a museum. I hate museums, anyway."

"If a museum wants what has been found—I'm sure that more than one would like your spoon, Jenny—they will pay for it and the law says that the finder must be paid full value."

"I see. If you find it you have to give it up, but then you may be paid a lot of money. Do you want a lot of money, Mr Wilkins? Is that your trouble? Dad says that it's his trouble—not enough of it, I mean."

"It is not my main trouble, my child. All my life I have studied this subject, and I want nothing more now than to be left alone to go on with my exploration in my own way and in my own time . . . Since my wife died I have no home of my own. I wish to find something which will add to our knowledge and understanding of the past."

There was a knock on the door and Mr Harman came in.

"Excuse me, Mr Wilkins, but it is time that Jenny was in bed. Thank you for entertaining her."

The old man nodded.

"The thanks should come from me, Mr Harman. And an apology to you, I think, for my behaviour this afternoon. You will forgive me, I am sure, if I say no more than that I am anxious to spend my holiday in these parts without interference from others, even should they be relations. Good night, Mr Harman . . . And good night to you, Jenny."

Jenny paused at the door.

"Good night, Mr Wilkins . . . And don't you worry about a thing. We'll all look after you, and if you'll allow it we'll help you search for treasure trove too. You've no idea how useful we can be . . ."

And later, when her head was at last on her pillow, she remembered her spoon. She turned over, put out her hand and felt her treasure hanging on its ribbon from the chair by her bed.

4. Enter Percy

EARLY NEXT MORNING Witchend was bustling with activity as the Lone Piners prepared for the camping holiday. Peter had come down to help and unbelievably the cavalcade started off to time. In the front of the car with Mr Morton was Peter, while David, the twins and Macbeth were squashed into the back with Tom, who was waiting at Ingles with his rucksack.

They had travelled perhaps ten miles and were approaching a fairly sharp bend to the left when there came the imperious sound of a horn not very far behind them. Mr Morton glanced in the driving mirror and signalled the car behind him to slow down and not attempt to pass him on the bend. But the driver of the big car in the rear must have been in a great hurry, for he kept his finger on the horn. Mr Morton signalled again that he should keep his place, and applied his own brakes for the corner, and just as Peter said, "There are some motor horns I hate. This sounds loud and expensive and, anyway, the driver is very rude," Mr Morton realized that the stranger was coming up fast on his right and attempting to pass him on the corner. He put his hand on the horn and braked harder as a long, sleek, pale-green car, pulling a caravan, drew ahead and then suddenly cut in sharply across his bonnet. Mr Morton drew in farther to the left of the road and felt his wheels lurch on the grass verge and then slip sideways into the narrow ditch.

When Mr Morton got out his face was white with rage. The green car was already nearly out of sight, and behind him their own trailer had one wheel in the ditch and had almost overturned. Tom and David followed him, and after uncoupling it, soon had it on the road.

"Thanks, boys," Mr Morton said. "Now I'll get our car out properly and we'll couple up again if there's no other damage done, and I don't think there is . . . I'd like to meet that fellow again, for in all my experience I don't think I've ever seen worse driving or worse manners . . . Did you get his number, Peter?"

She shook her head ruefully. "I'm sorry. I'll never forget the car, though. I'd know it anywhere, wouldn't you, David?"

"Sure of it. I'd know the caravan too."

"If ever I see that car again I'll stick my knife in all four tyres," Dickie remarked between clenched teeth.

"It's not often I take a real dislike to anyone," Tom added, "but I saw that chap's face as he went by, and I tell you that he was enjoying himself. He thinks he's clever . . . and the caravan looked like a hotel on wheels . . . He would have one like that . . ."

None of them had much to say for the next ten miles. The winding road along which they were travelling was densely wooded on their left, but beyond the trees was the bulk of the Stiperstones, and they knew that they were only a mile or so from Barton Beach.

Mr Morton was taking a right-hand turn when Peter suddenly said excitedly.

"Please stop a minute. We've caught up with them."

Mr Morton braked and pulled in. About fifty yards ahead, just where a track through the wood met the road, was the green car and the caravan.

"Ah!" Mr Morton said, "this is very fortunate. I shall enjoy a word with that gentleman! But I think perhaps you had all better stay here, because what I have to say is not fit for young ears."

Mary leaned forward from the back of the car.

"Let us approach with stealth, Daddy. I bet they're up to something beastly, and I'd like to catch them at it. I'm sure I can see them standing under the trees."

"Let's have a lingering revenge," Dickie echoed. "Let's make them pray for mercy and then not do it—the mercy, I mean."

"They are up to something peculiar," Peter said as she got out and stood on the edge of the road. "I think they're arguing about something . . . Tell you what, David. If we could get the car up nearer without them noticing, will you slip out with me, hide behind their caravan and see what's happening? I'd like to know what they're doing. Looks as if there's a boy there and someone else as well."

Mr Morton smiled. "You're as bad as Jenny, Peter, but I think it's not a bad idea."

The twins protested that they were being left out again, but Tom whispered that it was their particular job to keep Mackie quiet as their car slid silently forward.

About ten yards from the strangers Mr Morton stopped and switched off the engine, and Peter and David stepped quietly out on to the road. Now they could hear voices— ugly voices—raised in argument as, on tiptoe, they crept closer until, hidden behind the back of the caravan, they were able to relax and listen.

A man's voice first—"Now just you listen to me, Uncle. You don't want to be wandering about this country by yourself! You know you don't. You know you're not well enough and that you'll only do yourself harm if you go racketing around here all on your own looking for old things and the like. You might be ill again with one of your bad heads and then where would you be without those that's used to caring for you and—and—cherishing you!" he finished unexpectedly.

Peter looked at David in astonishment. The voice, apart from the words of the speaker, was certainly very unpleasant.

Then came an answer—querulous and unhappy. The voice of an old man.

"Just let me alone, Herbert. It's not much I ask of you at any time, but now I beg you both to go away and leave me here. I was happy enough until you came, and well looked after. Please go away."

At this David, who was nearer the side of the road,

pulled Peter closer to him, and they both peered round the side of the caravan.

Just at the side of the track which led up through the trees was a gnarled hawthorn tree, against which an old man was standing. He was, of course, Jenny's friend, Mr Wilkins, and he looked frightened.

Three people stood facing him, and at first glance Peter found it difficult to decide which looked the most unpleasant. The man was heavily built and dark complexioned. Although probably under middle age, he was plump with good living, and even from where they stood David and Peter could see grease glistening on his black hair. He was wearing a buff-coloured sports jacket above smartly-creased checked trousers. A cigar was held between his full lips, and a large ring sparkled on the little finger of his left hand.

Behind him was a small woman wearing a scarlet dress, a short fur coat and white shoes. Rings sparkled from her fingers and pearls encircled her throat. Her voice was shrill and ugly, reminding Peter of a parrot, as she said:

"You know perfectly well that you promised to spend your holidays with us, Uncle, and you know quite well that Percy here is ready to help you search for those old things you hope to find . . . You know you can't do all this by yourself. We want to help you, Uncle . . . Reely we do, you know . . . Why won't you join up with us like you said and let Percy help you? . . . You know how clever he is, Uncle dear."

Uncle dear regarded his great-nephew with undisguised revulsion, and so did David and Peter. Percy was quite unlike any boy they had ever seen before. He might have been thirteen, but it was difficult to tell, as he was tall and thin. Any normal boy on holiday in the country, Peter thought, would be in casual clothes. This boy was wearing a double-breasted flannel suit. His face was white, and while his parents were talking he was idly kicking stones in the direction of Mr Wilkins's unprotected ankles.

"There's only one person Percy is likely to help," Peter

whispered with her mouth against David's ear, "and that's Percy. What shall we do now?"

"Quiet for just a minute longer," David begged, making signs behind his back to the others in the car. "Listen. They're at him again."

"Now do stop this nonsense, Uncle," the man said. "We can't stop here all day now we have found you. Come back with us now and we'll have a nice cosy chat together about your ideas of finding something valuable round here, and then we'll all work together and help you . . . All we got to do is to co-operate and be business-like."

"But I don't want to be business-like," Mr Wilkins pleaded. "There's nothing I hate more. That's why I want to have my holiday by myself in my own way. I never meant you to come with me. It's only once a year I can go away and be by myself and do what I want to do. Please go now and stop that boy kicking stones at me . . . I like it here and I like wandering round by myself—and besides, I've found a friend."

The man stepped forward and put his hand on the lapel of the old man's coat.

"And what else have you found? That's what we want to know. What else have you found, slinking round these woods like the greedy old wolf you are? No more of this now . . . What have you found?"

Just as David moved forward from behind the caravan a noise from the road made them all turn. Mackie had jumped from Mary's restraining arms through the open window of the car and rushed up to David, barking wildly. The three bullies turned at once, but not before Peter had seen the old man cringe at the way in which he had just been questioned.

Then the twins and Tom jumped out of the car and walked towards the caravan, while Mr Morton was getting out of the driving seat.

"Come here, Mackie," David yelled as the little dog pranced menacingly towards the group under the trees.

But the gallant Macbeth pretended not to hear. Down

he went on his forepaws like a miniature black lion, and terrifying growls rumbled in his throat.

Percy never hesitated. He stooped, picked up the largest stone within reach, and flung it with all his strength at the dog. He was too near to miss and Mackie yelped with pain as the stone glanced off his thick coat.

Then a lot of things happened. Dickie and Mary, speechless with fury, dashed forward as David picked up the dog and ran back with him to his father.

"Shut him in the car, Dad. I don't think he's hurt much, but that brat might have killed him . . . I'll tackle this chap now."

While Mr Morton, who did not seem to realize that he was being ordered about by his own son, turned back obligingly with the squirming and furious little dog under his arm, David and Peter faced the enemy. The boy fidgeted a little uneasily as Peter fixed him with her eye, the woman's mouth fell open and the man began to bluster.

"What's all this about? What do you kids want? What's the idea?"

"Did you see what that boy did to our dog?" Peter began, but David put a hand on her arm and broke in, "Just a sec, Peter." Then to the man, "My father would like a word with you in a minute, sir. We've been looking for you . . . I suppose you know you nearly killed us all just now by passing us on a corner and forcing us into the ditch?"

The man flushed. "Nonsense, boy. No such thing. Never done such a thing. Must have been somebody else. You're mistaken."

"Oh, no, we're not," Peter flashed. "I'd know your car anywhere and that caravan too. We've got your number and there were plenty of witnesses."

"Get out of 'ere," the man shouted, and then stopped in amazement at the sight of the twins hurling themselves at his precious Percy. Just behind came Tom, who grabbed them as Percy turned, ready to fly to the shelter of the wood.

There was a brief and undignified scuffle during which

Mary, to her everlasting shame, kicked Tom on the ankle. He grinned and said:

"No good fighting the wrong man, Mary . . . Just go steady, because he's ready to run away. Just what you'd expect from a chap who throws stones at little dogs."

Mary turned and, with an odd gesture, touched his cheek.

"Sorry, Tom . . . All right, Dickie . . . Let's *tell* him what we think of him. Listen, you beastly little bully. You might have killed our dog. I believe you tried to kill him and we'll never, never, NEVER forget what you did. We'll find out who you are and we'll follow you wherever you go, and if Mackie is really hurt my father will help us to send you to prison—"

Tom's hand was fortunately still on Dickie's collar as he jumped forward with clenched fists.

"You're bigger'n me. 'Bout six inches. Take off your jacket and fight me now . . . I dare you to . . . Come on! Come and knock me about instead of throwing stones at little dogs . . . So you won't? Maybe you'd rather fight my sister Mary here, but she'd lick you with one hand behind her back . . . Do you see that, Tom? He's afraid. I knew he would be."

Percy, quite obviously, was afraid. He licked his lips and muttered something about "Stupid, common little kids," and backed away a few steps up the track.

While all this was going on Mr Morton, rather amused, was leaning against the bonnet of his car. It had not taken him long to judge the type of person with whom they had to deal, he had the number of the car, he was certain Mackie was not seriously hurt, and he trusted the Lone Piners to be a match for any hooligans. But while David stood by Tom and the twins, Peter slipped by the Smithsons—for the bullies were the Smithsons, of course—and walked quietly up to the pathetic Mr Wilkins.

When Peter tried to be friendly and charming few could resist her, and when she smiled at old Mr Wilkins and said, "Good morning! I'm sure you must be a friend of our friend Jenny Harman. Aren't you staying with her at Barton

Beach?" he looked a little happier and tried a smile in return.

"Indeed I am, young lady, but I have no idea how you could know."

"Never mind about that, Mr Wilkins. But do, please, understand that we are all friends of Jenny and we're on our way to meet her and go camping ... Would you like to come with us now?"

The old man looked at her with interest and smiled again. Then he glanced at the noisy group twenty yards away, and winced a little as Mr Smithson left the twins and came towards him. Peter had her back to the road and was not sure why Mr Wilkins did not answer her question.

"There's plenty of room, Mr Wilkins. Why don't you come with us?" Then she dropped her voice. "We've really come to help you. Jenny did tell you we were on our way, didn't she? Come with us now, please!"

The approaching Smithson heard the last appeal. His face was scarlet with rage as he turned on Mr Wilkins and snarled, "Be quiet, you!" Then, "Now, my girl, we've had enough of this. Don't know who you are or what you want, but I'll trouble you to mind your own business and clear out ... Understand?"

Peter looked at him scornfully.

"Don't you dare to touch me," she said. "Put your hands down."

Smithson changed his tactics. He tried to smile at her and said quietly:

"Fact is, my dear, the old chap is not quite—you know, not quite well. He's in our charge, you see, and you mustn't take too much notice of what he says."

Peter turned her back on him.

"If you'd like to come to Barton now, right away, with us, Mr Wilkins, you'll be very welcome."

She stood waiting for him to reply and, by an odd coincidence, the shouting and wrangling a few yards away stopped at that moment and it was almost as if everyone was waiting for his answer. Then, to his own and everyone else's surprise, he looked up and said a little fearfully, "Thank you, my dear. That is very courteous of you. I shall be glad to accept your offer."

"But you can't do that," Smithson blustered. "Come back, you stupid old fool."

Mr Wilkins put a hand on Peter's shoulder and walked steadily ahead, ignoring Mrs Smithson and Percy.

"This is Mr Wilkins, David," Peter said as they joined him. "He's coming with us to Barton."

David smiled and nodded before running back to tell his father. The twins and Tom were just as quick to see what was happening, and immediately formed a bodyguard for the old man.

When they reached the road Mr Morton shook hands with Mr Wilkins and made him welcome.

"I understand from Petronella that you would like a lift into Barton at once. Delighted to help . . . Mary! Remove this dangerous dog from the car now and help this gentleman in . . . Don't whisper like that, Dickie. Speak out. I'm sure you wouldn't say anything you didn't want anyone else to hear."

"Wouldn't I?" Dickie protested. "You bet I would. I can think of a hundred things. Anyway, what I was going to say was that Mary and me and Mackie would like to walk. It can't be far to Barton and we'd rather enjoy it—*partickerly* as you'll want to get off in a hurry," he added, with a wink of tremendous significance.

Mr Smithson was now so angry that he could hardly speak as he came up to the car. But he was no match for Mr Morton, who pretended at first not to notice him as he got into the driving seat. "Is it all right to leave those twins?" Peter whispered. "I mean—won't these awful people attack them or something?"

Mr Morton laughed. "Much more likely that the twins will attack them. They'll be all right, Peter. I wish I could stay and watch the fun."

He leaned from the window. "So long, you two. It shouldn't take you long to walk, and I'll wait there for you

before I start back again." Then he nodded pleasantly to
Smithson. "Good morning. You will be hearing from me
later," and let in the clutch.

It was all too easy for the twins. They just stood around
and watched the Smithsons, and moved when they moved.
They stared at them until they fidgeted, and when they
saw Mr Smithson's fists clenching and unclenching at his
sides they were particularly glad they had decided to stay
behind.

They behaved with scrupulous politeness and pretended
not to hear Percy's nasty little remarks, but they watched
them all the time until at last they got back into the green
car. Then they stepped forward together and smiled upon
the sulky Percy.

"We shall see you again, dear Percy," Mary whispered.

"You've got a surprise coming, you dirty little snivelling
bully," Dickie muttered. "We'll never forget you, and
neither will Mackie."

When the car was out of sight they looked at each other
and laughed.

"That was fun," was all that Dickie said.

Then Mary protested that it was too hot to start walking
on the road to Barton.

"If we wait long enough," she said reasonably, "Daddy
will come back and fetch us. I feel like exploring this little
wood. This track leads somewhere interesting, I'm
sure."

Dickie could never resist doing something unplanned, so
very willingly they turned up the track. After a hundred
yards they found themselves at the foot of a deep and
sinister-looking valley. Although grass, bracken and heather
were growing on the lower slopes and round the stony bed
of a stream which twisted sharply away from them to the
left instead of following the track through the wood, the
"feel" of the place was forbidding. Two black-and-white
magpies flapped out of the trees and up the valley, and then
Dickie pointed upwards and said, "I thought so, Mary.
There's that old Devil's Chair up on the top. This is one of

the Stiperstone dingles, and I don't like it much. What shall we do?"

Mary looked puzzled. "I know it's silly, but I think I've been here before . . . Or do you think it's just one of those odd feelings you get sometimes? You know what I mean, don't you, Dickie?"

Her twin nodded. "I know, but I haven't got this feeling yet. Let's go on—just round the corner, so that we can see farther ahead—and then come back. What do two magpies mean?"

"Jenny would know. I think maybe it's 'two for joy,' but I don't feel that's coming true . . . Come on."

The mountain towered above them on their right, and as they trudged on they reminded each other of the *Seven White Gates* adventure, and of how they had been trapped in an old mine in the heart of the mountain. At the next turn in the valley Mary stopped suddenly.

"Look, twin! See that dark blob up there on the right— like a dark circle on the cliff? That's our cave, twin. The cave that leads right inside the mine. I knew I'd been here before."

They clambered up and stood again on the pleasant grassy plateau. The cave was just the same, but they did not go in far, as they had no ropes nor lights, and it was when they were standing again in the open looking up and down the wild valley that Dickie had his great idea.

"Let's make this our camping place, Mary. It's just right, for we've got the cave if it's wet and this grass for the tents if it's fine—and there's water in the stream just below. Let's hurry back now and tell the others."

Mary agreed that this was an idea worthy of them and, a little reluctantly, they turned their backs on the cave.

"There's something funny about this stream, Dickie," she said when they had scrambled down from the plateau. "You said just now there was plenty of water here for the camp, but the stream seems to disappear just here. Where is it?"

And Mary was right, for they noticed now that although

61

it looked as if water might once have run along the stony bed, it was certainly dry now.

"But we *saw* the stream lower down," Dickie protested. "Let's see if it's running higher up."

Mary looked anxious.

"I'm thinking about Daddy, twin. We've been a long time, and he'll be mad if he can't find us when he comes back. Let's come and look tomorrow."

Dickie protested that another five minutes would make no difference, so they hurried up the dingle again, but it was a quarter of a mile before they found a large pool into which the little stream was tumbling.

"It comes in, but doesn't run out properly," Dickie said. "This is all very rum."

"I s'pose it runs underground," Mary said. "It must do, because it isn't even overflowing, but I s'pose we could get water from this pool."

Then they trotted back down the valley and found that, as Mary had guessed, the stream ran only occasionally on the surface of the valley. Twice it bubbled up through the stones into a pool, ran for some distance along its original bed, and then disappeared underground again. Mary had great difficulty in dragging her twin away from these pools.

"It's no use, Mary. I like water. I like mucking about in it. Let's make sure we come back tomorrow."

They hurried through the wood to the road and were rather relieved to find that their father was not waiting for them, but they were very tired and footsore when they did meet him, as Mary had anticipated, half a mile along the road to Barton.

"You've been a long time getting as far as this," Mr Morton said as he turned the car. "What have you been up to? Everything all right? No trouble with those people?"

Mary climbed in beside him and passed Macbeth to Dickie in the back.

"You are the very nicest father," she said. "We want you to know how we 'preciate it."

"Thank you very much," Mr Morton said gravely; "but what have you been up to? No trouble?"

They explained how the Smithsons had driven off in a rage and that they had been exploring and found a camping place, and soon after they were greeting the others and Jenny at the post office.

Mrs Harman, for once, was genial and expected them all to stay to tea. Jenny was almost speechless with excitement, for never before had she been able to entertain so many friends at the same time in her own home.

"I must get back to Witchend," Mr Morton said at last, "and you must all get out of Mrs Harman's way and give her some peace. I don't know whether you've made any plans as to where you're going to camp tonight—"

"Yes, we have," the twins said. "We've found the very place, but we're afraid you'll have to tow the trailer back some of the way."

The others looked at them pityingly and their father went on: "I know you told me you'd found a camp site, but it's too late to start your permanent camp now. Why don't you all go up to Seven Gates and ask Mr Sterling and Charles whether you can use that old barn just for tonight?"

And while they all, except the twins, looked at him with admiration, he turned to Mr Wilkins.

"Good-bye, Mr Wilkins. Glad we were able to help you today. I must apologize for these children and their noise, but I promise that you can trust them. Don't let them be a nuisance, but allow them to help you if they can. They know this country round here."

They all trooped down to see him off, and when the car had disappeared David said:

"That's a grand idea. You'll come too, won't you, Jenny, and stay the night with us?"

Jenny was doubtful. "I'm sure Mum will let me come, but do you think we ought to leave Mr Wilkins? He's been very quiet since you brought him back. I don't think I'll stay the night at Seven Gates. I think it best to guard Mr

Wilkins until we really make our plans. I'll come up with you all if I may though."

"She's like a small bird looking after a cuckoo," Peter laughed.

"Listen!" Dickie shouted in despair, "NOW will you listen to us about the camp we've found?"

"No, little man, we will not," David said. "We'll listen to you at supper—that is, if you've got the strength to talk, for you've got to pull the trailer up to H.Q.2 . . . Let's get going."

Later when they were on their way, hauling the trailer, Jenny suddenly stopped.

"Don't wait for me," she said. "I won't be long. I've forgotten something," and she ran back along the village street, through the shop and up the stairs, and knocked on the door of Mr Wilkins's room.

"It's only me—Jenny," she gulped. "Please may I come in?"

He was standing by the window and she saw the sad look in his eyes as he turned to greet her.

"What is it, child?"

"Nothing much," she said shyly. "Just that I want you to know I'm coming back home tonight and we're all coming tomorrow like we promised. Don't worry about anything, will you, Mr Wilkins? We'll have the most marvellous fun tomorrow and help you to explore and do everything you want . . . Just you rely on us," and she ran out of the room and down the stairs again.

5. Seven Gates

Jenny soon caught up with the Lone Pine procession on its way to Seven Gates. Progress was necessarily slow for the trailer was heavy, and when Peter looked back over her shoulder and saw Jenny coming up the road behind them she waited for her.

"Forget something, Jen?"

"Not really. I just wanted to comfort Mr Wilkins. Oh! Look! . . . The boys have stopped . . . They look annoyed."

And so they were. Both David and Tom, who were pulling the trailer up the hill, were scarlet in the face and almost too breathless with their exertions to speak. But not so the twins, who were supposed to be pushing behind.

"Thank you *very* much, Peter and Jenny," Mary protested. "Don't you bother about us. You just go off and have a nice gossip somewhere while we——"

"Break our backs and blister our hands, and wear out our shoes to the bone!" Dickie added. "Are you two in this party or not?"

"Sorry, David," Peter smiled. "Now you and Tom have got it over the top of the hill we'll give a hand . . . I just wanted a word with Jenny. Now let's hurry. I want to give them all a surprise."

"I should think we'll do that," David agreed. "Neither your father nor your uncle know what's coming to them yet, and I shudder to think what your nice Aunt Carol will say. . . . Come on, then. Let's get going."

They passed the first lane on the right of the road and soon came to the second, and then, within five minutes, were climbing again and had reached the shadow of the whispering trees. The first white gate swung open easily when the latch was lifted.

"These hinges used to squeak," Peter remarked, "but everything is different on the farm now that Charles is back."

The second gate was the same and so was the third, which opened on the big farmyard. Over by one of the barns a tall, good-looking man in brown corduroys and a checked shirt turned to see who was coming to Seven Gates at this time of the evening.

Then, "Bless us all," he drawled, with a flash of white teeth, "it's a circus! Hi, Peter! Hi, Jenny, and hello, twins and all! . . . Are you staying long with all that gear?" and he strolled across to greet them as Mary dashed forward and flung her arms round his legs.

"We've come twenty weary miles to see you, dear Charles. How are you after all this time?"

"Seems as if you're moving house! . . . How's young Richard? And David and Tom?"

He shook hands all round, and when David tried to explain he interrupted and said:

"Don't break the news yet! Come in and see everyone."

"Welcome, Petronella, and welcome to all her friends. Come in!" Micah Sterling's voice boomed out as they trooped through the door.

Peter smiled as she slipped past him in the narrow hall and rushed up to the little man waiting in the background.

"Daddy! It's me. I'm back again, and we're going camping, but we want to stay in the old barn to night. How are you?"

Then Mrs Sterling joined in the welcome, and it was five minutes before any of them could hear themselves speak. At last Peter explained that, more than anything else, they wanted to camp in the old barn.

"And we've brought most of our food, Aunt Carol," Peter continued, "and our rugs and sleeping-bags, but if we could light up the old stove and camp there again just till the morning it would be grand . . . You don't mind, do you, Uncle Micah?"

"Ask Charles," the old man smiled. "He is the master here now."

Charles had no objection.

66

"You boys come with me now," he said, "and help me clear out some of the junk, and you can camp in there as long as you like."

"Come to supper with us, Charles," Peter pleaded, and was thrilled when he accepted the invitation.

The old barn in the corner of the farmyard was vaulted and pillared like a church. Once it had been used for the storage of grain, and each side was partitioned off into sections, which were used by the Lone Piners as bedrooms. At the far end an almost vertical stairway led up to another granary under the sloping roof, and here, close by the little window that looked over the tree-tops to Barton Beach, Peter and Mary chose to sleep.

By the foot of the stairway on the ground floor was an old iron stove, round which the campers sat in the evenings and on which they tried to do their cooking.

Within fifteen minutes the barn had been cleared, the floor had been swept, the trailer unloaded and the fire lit. Then they built up the old trestle-table, borrowed two long polished benches and lit the hanging hurricane lamps. Peter was cook, and with Jenny to run to and fro for her, and with Mrs Sterling's help, sausages and eggs were soon frizzling in the old iron frying-pan on the top of the stove. While the cooks were at work, Mary unpacked the sleeping-bags and blankets, and ran off to persuade Charles to let them have some hay for bedding. Macbeth disgraced himself by chasing two of the farm cats out of the farmyard, while David and Tom checked up to see if they had really brought everything they needed.

Meanwhile, Dickie had found a piece of white cardboard on which he printed:

> H.Q.2.
>
> PRIVIT.
>
> KEEP OUT!

and pinned it very carefully to the door of the barn.

It was dark when the twins and Tom eventually went over to the house—the former to fetch their guest and the latter to carry over a big jug of hot cocoa which was Mrs Sterling's contribution to the feast.

Later, when the meal was over, Charles lit his pipe.

"Thanks, Lone Piners," he smiled; "that was grand . . . Now tell me the big idea. Why have you come here, for I guess you're up to something—and don't all look so innocent! All except Jenny, that is. Her eyes are popping out of her head with excitement . . . Are you going to tell me or is it a secret?"

"Let's tell him," Jenny whispered hoarsely. "Let's not hide anything from Charles. He's one of us really."

Charles got up and bowed.

"Thanks a lot, Jenny. That was nobly said. I'm down-right proud."

"Don't imagine you're a real member of this club just because of that, Charles," Peter laughed. "You're much too old, but if you behave yourself and help us when we want you, maybe we'll make you an honorary member one day!"

"I vote we tell Charles about today," Mary said. "I don't think I could ever bear to keep a secret from him," she added with a sigh. "But, after all, we haven't got a real secret yet, have we? Let's ask him what he thinks about Jenny's Mr Wilkins and the nasty Smithsons."

So they pushed back the trestle-table, pulled the two benches round the stove, and while Peter shared out the remains of the cocoa, Jenny was persuaded to tell her story. As soon as she forgot her shyness she told it well, but Charles, still puffing at his old pipe, did not say anything until the twins had added their tale of the Smithsons' discomfiture.

"—An' what we did to them is just nothing at all, really," Dickie finished. "We mean it's nothing to what we'd like to do. We think they are the beastliest people we've ever met—"

"Did we tell you the boy's name?" Mary broke in. "It's

Percy. Really it is. Acksherly PERCY! An' he flung a mighty rock at poor Mackie, and *one day* dear Percy is goin' to have a big surprise!"

"But what we really want to ask you, Charles," David said, "is whether you think this old chap Wilkins may be right and that Jenny's silver spoon is genuine and that there might be some Roman treasure to be found round here . . . We are going to make a camp somewhere in this area for a few days, anyway, but we don't want to get mixed up with Mr Wilkins if it's going to make trouble and if he's talking nonsense."

Before Charles could reply there was an interruption.

Jenny, scarlet in the face with indignation, broke in.

"David! I've never heard you say anything so *awful* . . . I want to say right now that even if poor old Mr Wilkins is talking nonsense, I don't mind getting mixed up with him. I'm not going to desert him now, whatever anybody else says or does, and if the Club is afraid of trouble then I'm not . . . I've just promised that we're all going to help him. He's miserable and unhappy and alone, and I never heard such a beastly thing to say—"

Poor David put a hand to his forehead in despair.

"I'm sorry, Jenny. I didn't mean that exactly but it's such a rum story, and we do want to know where we are, don't we?"

"No, we don't," Tom said. "I'm with Jen."

"Steady! Steady!" Charles said. "David is right to try and keep a clear head over all this, and Jenny and Tom are right to stick to friends whatever happens but if you'll all be quiet for a few minutes I'll tell you what I think.

"First of all, whatever you decide to do, you must remember that what is going on between old man What's-his-Name and this unpleasant nephew is nothing to do with you, and you must not interfere in their relationship . . . BUT—if he asks you to help him scratch about in the dingles round here, I can't see why you shouldn't. I haven't met him yet, but there's nothing crazy in his idea that the Romans once lived up in this country. We know they did.

69

You can still walk along the straight road they made in the Stretton valley over by your place, Peter, and we know that they mined for lead in these very hills. Jenny tells us that the old chap seems serious in his belief that he can find something valuable, and for all that I know he may be right . . . As for this spoon that you found at Bishop's Castle, it might be a good idea if you took it to the museum in Shrewsbury. If they thought it was genuine that would prove that Mr Wilkins knew what he was talking about, wouldn't it?"

"Even a genuine Roman spoon found at Bishop's Castle market doesn't prove much," David objected. "I mean it doesn't prove that it was dug up round here, does it? It might have been brought from anywhere and nobody knows how it got on to the junk stall where Jenny first saw it."

"It doesn't prove much," Charles agreed, "but I still think it is a good idea. Would you trust me to take the spoon to Shrewsbury, Jenny?"

"I'll trust you, of course, but I'm not going to let it go. I believe Mr Wilkins, and I think we're going to have an adventure because of it, but I don't want anyone else to know about it yet. If we take it to a museum lots of fussy grown-ups will get excited and interfere, and everything will be spoiled . . . Maybe I'll take it along one day. But not now."

"I agree with Jen," Tom said stolidly, and did not look surprised even when everybody laughed.

"Very well," Charles said. "It's your spoon, Jenny, but I will tell you now that there have always been rumours of hidden treasure in these hills. Like Peter and Jenny, I was born and bred in Shropshire, and so was my father. When I was about the twins' age I remember tales he told me of this country. Most of you know these old stories, many of which are founded on fact."

"Tell us again, dear Charles," Mary begged.

And so, while the embers in the stove died down and the two hurricane lamps flickered over their heads, he reminded them that almost every hill in Shropshire has its ancient camp, and that there is more than one stone circle where our distant ancestors worshipped the sun god. He told them that only a few miles away Caractacus fought and lost the last great battle for British independence. He told them of Offa's Dyke and of how Edric the Saxon, after a gallant fight, surrendered to the Norman invader, and how his restless spirit still haunts the hills.

"Then there's the old Devil's Chair over our heads," he went on, "and Jenny knows there's plenty born and bred round here who put up the shutters when the mist comes up and hides those rocks. Maybe I'm used to this mountain now, for I see it every day and work under it, but like many others I know well there's something strange about it—some say 'tis a curse on all the land in its shadow . . . And that reminds me of another bad-luck yarn. I remember it as a kid, but someone told me it again the other day."

Jenny shivered with horrified delight.

"Go *on!*" Mary whispered.

"Some say there is a mysterious river somewhere in these hills—a river that is only seen on the surface at special times, and that when it does appear it flows without warning and brings bad luck to all who live within an hour's walking distance of its waters. Then there's another story—and this I believe to be true—of an underground waterway which was built originally to drain one of the mines and later used as a sort of subterranean canal to carry loads of minerals from the mines . . . Maybe the last story accounts for the first. I don't know for certain, except that it is likely enough that the miners of a hundred years ago knew all about it and passed the story down. Have you ever heard that, Jenny?"

"I seem to remember Dad once saying something about water that came out of a mine a mile or more away. Please, somebody tell me the time, 'cos I think I ought to have been home hours ago."

Charles looked at his watch.

"Ten o'clock!" he said. "Bed-time. Thanks for the party,

and I'll see you all in the morning. I don't want to interfere, but if I can do anything to help let me know. Good night, all."

David and Peter followed him to the big doors of the barn and watched him cross the farmyard. Then the latter turned to Jenny and said:

"I s'pose you *must* go home tonight, Jen? It's awfully late and it's a long way down, although the moon will be up soon . . . Stay and sleep with Mary and me upstairs, and then you can slip home before seven in the morning."

"I couldn't do that, Peter. Really I couldn't. I'd love to stay, but I promised Mr Wilkins—and Mum and Dad too, of course—that I'd be back. I must go—but I wish I needn't," she added with a scared glance outside.

"I'll come with you, Jen," Tom said suddenly. "I'd be glad to stretch my legs."

"We'll all come," David agreed; "it'll do us good. This place is getting stuffy. Put some wood on the stove, Peter, and the twins can stay and keep an eye on it."

"*Can* they?" Dickie said as he wriggled into a sweater. "It can keep an eye on itself because we're coming too. And so is Mackie."

The moon came up as soon as they had left the trees behind them, but it was a watery moon and often hidden behind scudding clouds. The fresh air made them forget how sleepy they had been ten minutes ago, and they were all arm-in-arm and singing when they reached the top of Barton's only street.

"This is fun," Jenny said, "and I think it's wonderful of you all to come with me, but I do hate that wood even in the day-time. I'll be all right now if you want to go back."

"We'll come all the way now," Peter said.

"Maybe we'd better not make so much noise," David added. "Everybody in this place seems to have gone to bed . . . I wish you twins would walk in front. We keep on tripping over you in the dark."

The twins, obedient for once, went on ahead for a few paces with Mackie trotting sedately beside them, and for a minute or so it was only the sound of six different footsteps which broke the silence of the sleeping village. The moon slid up above the rooftops and splashed one side of the street with silver.

Suddenly the twins stopped, but when David trod on Dickie's heel he did not complain, but only turned to look over his shoulder.

"That was a boy," Mary whispered. "Did you see him too, Dickie? He was creeping along right up against the wall of that house on the other side of the street. Did you see him, David?"

Her elder brother shook his head, but Dickie said, "I saw him, twin! He was slinking. He's gone down what looks like a narrow passage between the houses. Is there a passage there, Jenny?"

"Oh, yes. It leads to a lane."

"That was dear, beautiful, beloved Percy," Mary whispered. "I'm sure it was. Come on, twin! Let's see where he's going."

"Come back, you little idiots!" David tried to shout in a whisper. "It's too late to start that now."

"Don't worry about us," Dickie called softly as they ran across the road with Mackie at their heels. "We'll find out something. Don't follow us or anything, 'cos that will make too much noise. Go straight back and we'll follow you to H.Q.2 soon as we can. 'Night, Jenny. See you in the morning."

Peter laughed. "Don't worry, David; they'll be all right. They know the way back, and if it was Percy it will be useful to know where he's sleeping and what he's doing."

Tom shrugged his shoulders and walked on ahead with Jenny. He often lost patience with the twins.

"I suppose they can't get lost," David said to Peter as they followed the others up the street, "and it would be stupid for us all to go."

They said "good night" to Jenny as soon as they found that the back door of the post office was unlocked, and after some further argument at the entrance to the passage down which the twins had disappeared, they decided to go back to the barn and tidy up while waiting for them.

As they turned up the hill again Tom shivered.

"It's getting cold and very dark," he said. "See those clouds chasing across the moon." Five minutes later, when they reached the first white gate, the moon disappeared behind a great bank of black cloud and the first heavy drops of rain pattered on the tree-tops.

"I told you it would rain," Peter said. "I've smelled it all day. Shouldn't be surprised if we don't get a lot, which will be a nuisance, because I suppose we shall have to stick to H.Q.2 until it clears . . . Lucky we've got that place for a camp, anyway."

They had reached the second gate now. David whispered, "Listen!"

They stood still and strained their ears as the rain fell more heavily. Then Peter spoke.

"I heard it then. You're right, David. That was a dog barking, and I believe—"

"You think it was Mackie. So do I. I'm sure of it. That was his angry bark . . . What shall we do?"

The silence surged back for a second and then, with a murmur that soon became a roar, the clouds opened and the rain poured down in earnest.

6. The Caravan

As soon as the twins, with Macbeth at their heels, crossed the road and ran into the narrow passage down which Percy had disappeared, they forgot everything but the excitement of the chase. This side of the street was in deep shadow and the sudden shock of finding themselves in darkness checked them and for a moment they stood still.

Dickie whispered, "Can you hear anything? . . . I s'pose that *was* Percy, wasn't it?"

Mary's fingers closed round his arm and her lips, close to his ear, whispered, "There is someone in front of us. I'm sure it was Percy."

He strained his ears and just caught the faint sound of distant feet running. Then Mackie, whose rough coat he could feel against his bare legs, growled softly.

"I can hear him," Dickie said, "but he seems to have got a good start . . . Come on, Mary. Let's see where this path leads."

Hand in hand they groped their way forward in the dark until they left the houses behind and realized that the track now ran between two gardens. The fitful moon helped them a little and before long the track became an unpaved lane with a high hedge on each side.

"I s'pose we just go straight on," Mary whispered, "but keep a lookout your side, twin. He may have squeezed through the hedge . . . Come here, Mackie."

"Better carry him," Dickie said. "I'm sure he knows that was Percy and I don't want him to give the game away . . . Hold him tight, Mary, and if he begins to growl you must gag him."

"Don't worry. I'll explain everything to him as we go along. He'll be all right. You go ahead, Dickie."

It was still dark between the high hedges, and as they went on as quickly and as quietly as they could they were both thinking what they would like to do to Percy one day.

The Morton twins were, perhaps, not fonder of animals than most children, but they had a tremendous sense of loyalty to each other and to their family and friends, and they counted Mackie very definitely as part of the family. Besides, they hated cruelty—particularly cruelty to animals or to someone weaker or not so happy as themselves—and even if Mackie had been rather quick to show his dislike of the Smithsons, to throw a stone at him from a few yards away was inexcusable.

After another twenty yards Dickie stopped suddenly.

"I can hear somebody talking . . . No, it's someone singing."

"It can't be, twin. There isn't a house near . . . Yes, it is! Now I can hear it . . . It's a radio, Dickie. That's what it is. . . . It's coming from over there."

Mackie growled as Dickie whispered, "I think we're coming to a gate or a gap in the hedge. Stay here, Mary, and keep Mackie quiet."

He was back in two minutes, his voice shaking with excitement.

"We were right, Mary. They're camping over in the corner of the next field. I can see the caravan 'cos it's all lighted up. The radio isn't as loud now, but I think we heard it when they opened the door to let Percy in."

"Let's creep quietly to the caravan and spy on them, and then decide what to do. I've been thinking over some plans, twin. I s'pose we couldn't set fire to the caravan—not when they are in it, o' course, though that's a pity really?"

Dickie looked at his twin with awe. He was usually responsible for the bloodthirsty suggestions in their partnership, and it seemed that he had underestimated her fury over the stone-throwing on this occasion.

"I hadn't thought of that," he admitted. "I don't really think that it's quite the sort of thing we ought to do, although o' course those beasts deserve it . . . But I hadn't thought of burning 'em up, twin . . . Not yet, anyway."

The meadow was large, and over in the far corner, under some trees, glowed the lighted windows of the caravan. They crept softly across the grass and when they were within ten yards they heard voices.

Mary clutched her brother's arm.

"It is," she breathed. "It really is them. I feel a bit sick, Dickie. Just with excitement. What shall we do?"

It was not often that Mary accepted her twin as the leader, but although Dickie's heart was thudding fiercely with just as much excitement, he responded to this trust at once.

"I'm going to try and look in through the window," he whispered. "I think it's too high for us, but if I can find something to stand on I could manage—and maybe I could hear what they're saying."

"You look and I'll listen," Mary said at once. "If I go to the door at the back and squat down close to it with Mackie, maybe I could hear something too."

Dickie nodded and crept forward and then squeezed under the caravan. His outstretched fingers touched wood, and although it was very heavy he managed to wriggle out backwards, dragging a large box after him. Very gently he pulled it under the window and then, with a sign of caution to Mary, who seemed to be struggling with Mackie, he stood on it and found that he could see into the caravan.

Mr Smithson was lying sprawled across a bunk with a glass of beer on the table before him, while his wife faced him with the back of her head only a few inches from the window. Facing his parents was Percy, who looked even more unpleasant than when Dickie had last seen him. His mean, sharp little face was pale, with a lock of dank hair falling across his forehead, and even while he was talking his jaws worked rhythmically on a wad of chewing-gum. And while he talked he waved his hands, and Dickie nearly collapsed with joy when he knocked his father's glass of beer off the table. As Mr Smithson grabbed at his drink he glanced towards the window, and with a stab of panic

77

Dickie bobbed down. Then he felt a hand on his arm, and Mary's voice, close to his ear, whispered, "I can't hear anything much, Dickie, except that they seem to be arguing and that Percy says, 'He done it.' Now let me up. I want to have a look. What can you see?"

"Mackie is shaking all over, Mary. He won't bark, will he? Do you think maybe we ought to go? We know where they are now, anyway, and we could come back in the morning."

"Mackie is all right, twin. I've got him. He's promised to be a good boy . . . Listen, Dickie. I want to be able to tell the others just exactly why Percy was prowling about the street. I b'lieve he's telling them now and I want to listen . . . Let me get up on the box," and before he could stop her she climbed up with Mackie still under her arm.

They were never quite sure what happened next, but as Dickie clutched at his sister to warn her to go carefully, it began to rain hard, and possibly the surface of the box was slippery, anyway. Mary lost her balance and as she put out her hand to lean on Dickie, Mackie squirmed out of her arms and began to bark furiously.

"*Be quiet*, Mackie," Mary pleaded. "Come here at once."

But Macbeth was tired of being carried even by Mary. He remembered the caravan and knew perfectly well that his enemies were inside it. So while the twins jumped off the box and ran towards him he gave tongue joyously and pranced out of reach, dodging round and under the caravan and voicing his defiance as the rain poured down even more heavily.

"Get under the caravan, twin," Dickie whispered urgently. "They'll come out. Don't let them see us," and they crawled into shelter as the door opened and Mr Smithson's voice called, "Anybody there?"

A golden light shone out into the rain from the open door, but Mackie very wisely kept out of its reach and continued to bark furiously in the darkness. Over his shoulder Smithson muttered, "Must be somebody about.

Or is it just a stray dog, d'you reckon? Sure you weren't followed here, Perce?"

Very faintly came the detested voice.

" 'Course I'm sure. Do you think I'm a fool, Pop?"

"What was it you was saying about those kids walking about all together in the street just when you done the job, eh? Did they see you and follow you here, Perce?"

"They couldn't have done. I was on the dark side and they were arm-in-arm, singing, going down towards the post office . . . I would have heard them if they come after me . . . All the same, I wish I knew what they were doing down there at that time . . ." Then his voice rose hysterically, "KEEP THAT DOG QUIET."

Just then Mackie, excited by Percy's outburst, bounded into the pool of light by the open door and barked more furiously than ever.

"It *is* their beastly little dog," Percy shouted. "I'd know it anywhere . . . You've got a gun in here, Pop . . . Shoot it!"

Under the caravan Dickie heard Mary's gasp of horror, and then, almost before he realized what was happening, he found himself dragged out into the rain. Mary's nails were biting into his wrist, but there was hardly a tremor in her voice as she called:

"Mackie! Come here at once, you naughty little dog! . . . But you're not *really* naughty, darling, because you've found someone for us at last . . . Oh, good evening. How do you do? Do you happen to remember us? We met earlier today by the side of the road after you had nearly killed us all at that corner!"

While she was talking, Mackie, rather ashamed now at his disobedience, sidled up with drooping tail and was grabbed into the safety of her arms. Mrs Smithson now poked herself forward so that her hard little face appeared at her husband's elbow.

"What are you two kids doing here?" she snapped. "Just be off with you as fast as you can run."

"Just a minute, dear," her husband said in a nasty, silky

sort of voice. "I don't think we should send these youngsters out in the rain at this time of night. I believe that would be very wrong. They're wet already, and I would like them to come and shelter until the storm is over. Perhaps a cup of tea would be good for us all . . . Come along in, you two."

The last five words were spoken in a very different tone of voice, and although Dickie had realized that Mary had shown themselves boldly to save Mackie, he was now equally sure that if they wanted to find out something about the Smithsons they would never have a better chance than this. All the same, he shivered a little at Mr Smithson's invitation to come into the caravan. It was rather like the spider and the fly!

"Come in," Smithson leered. "You're both getting wet out there. Come in and tell us what you're doing in this field at this time of night. We're curious to know."

Dickie's hand slid down Mary's sleeve and the touch of their fingers gave them each courage as it had so often done before.

"Thank you very much," he said clearly. "We are getting wet, and the truth is we are lost too."

"Utterly and completely lost," Mary took up the tale. "The others—and we're the smallest, you know—somehow got on ahead. It's 'cos we're little, you see. We can't walk as fast as them, an' Mackie here—"

"Have you seen our little dog before?" Dickie broke in. "How stupid of me! Of course you have. That boy threw a rock at him. You needn't be afraid of him now, because we'll hold him tight."

"If they've got to come in," Percy's sulky voice came from inside the caravan, "make the little beasts leave that vile dog outside."

Apparently Mr Smithson did not consider this to be a wise speech, although he was eyeing Macbeth with suspicion himself.

"No, thank you," Mary declined. "Mackie comes with me wherever I go. That's just the trouble. He was naughty and ran away, and then we started to look for him, and the

others didn't notice and we don't know where they are . . .
It's all very difficult for us, but we have found Mackie . . .
Do you really want us to come inside? How kind of you.
Come on, Dickie."

There was not really room for them all, but with an
innocent wriggle or two the twins managed to get their
backs to the closed door, and Dickie was happier when his
fingers touched the handle. Then he looked round curiously
and was interested to see, in a corner, an array of gleaming
tools—a pickaxe, several spades and shovels, and two or
three steel crowbars. When Percy noticed where his eyes
were wandering he scowled, but Dickie only smiled at him
sweetly.

"So you got lost in the dark, did you?" Mr Smithson
suddenly inquired. "Where were you off to at that time of
night?"

"Just a walk," Dickie explained with an airy wave of the
hand. "We like walks."

"Staying around here, are you? Far away?"

"Just around," Mary smiled. "Not far."

"How long will you be here, SIR?" Dickie said in his
very-best-manners voice. "I mean it's too dark for us to see
what sort of a field this is, but I suppose you must like it . . .
Has it got a nice view?"

"Impertinence!" Mrs Smithson snorted.

"Got friends around these parts?" Mr Smithson tried
again.

"Yes. Plenty," Mary agreed. "I expect some of them will
be coming to look for us soon."

"Staying with them are you? All your party, I suppose?
I was wondering why you chose this part of the country
for a holiday?"

Silence greeted this question until Dickie nodded in the
direction of the gleaming tools in the corner.

"I'd like to know," he said very distinctly, "whether
you've got anything to do with farmers or gardeners? Are
you all going to do a lot of digging? We loathe digging.
Mary and me, I mean. We're just not any good at it."

"Look here, kids," Mr Smithson said suddenly, "let's stop fooling. You remember that crazy old guy who went off in your father's car this afternoon? . . . 'Course you do, so it's no use shaking your heads. You know perfectly well who I mean. I want to know what he's got to do with your party."

"He's a friend," Dickie replied tersely.

"No, he's not," Mrs Smithson said. "He can't be. We know all his friends."

"No, you don't!" came from Mary. " 'Cos we are, and you don't know us."

"Never mind about that now," Smithson continued, and with joy they noticed that he was getting red in the face. "What I want you to tell me—and there'll be a bit of extra pocket money for you both if you do—is whether poor old Wilkins is staying at the post office, or is he still with the rest of your party?"

The twins looked at him blankly and there was a long silence.

The man tried again.

"What I want you children to understand," he gulped as he rather meaningly jingled some coins in his pocket, "is that you can help poor old Mr Wilkins by telling me what you know. Mr Wilkins isn't at all well, and we are looking after him . . . Now I know I'm talking to two very good and intelligent children who would like to make a little extra pocket money for themselves . . . Can you tell me where Mr Wilkins is now?"

"I s'pect he's in bed," Mary replied brightly. "If he's sensible that's where he is, and I wish I was there too. That's where we'd like to be, wouldn't we, twin?"

"Yes, we would. It sounds like it's still raining, but I think we'll go now, thank you very much."

"Not just yet," Mr Smithson said quietly. "You're not going from here until you've answered some questions. Where are you staying tonight? How far have you got to go?"

If they felt frightened at this threat they certainly did not

82

show it. Dickie felt the handle of the door sticking into his back and reckoned that it would not be very difficult to escape, and Mary fussed the little dog in her arms and said:

"We've got a very long way to go, thank you, and you wouldn't understand if we told you . . . Acksherly, we're staying with friends."

Mr Smithson suddenly changed his mind.

"I see," he said, and turned to his wife. "Mustn't keep 'em here if they want to go. That would be very wrong. Pass me my mack, dear, and I'll go along with them."

Dickie saw the trap at once and realized that Mr Smithson hoped that they would lead him to wherever they were staying. It occurred to him also that their enemy was particularly anxious to know whether they were all at the post office with Mr Wilkins. At the moment he could not quite see how they could prevent anyone following them if they went out into the rain, so, apart from leading Mr Smithson on a wild-goose chase all over the countryside, the best thing to do would be to stay where they were until they got an idea. And besides, they still had to find out what Percy had been doing in Barton.

Mary, as she so often did, seemed to know what he was thinking, for she looked up and said: "There's no need for you to get wet, thank you. We can manage quite well by ourselves when the rain stops . . ."

Then Percy spoiled his father's plan.

"Why don't you push 'em out in the wet when they've told you why they were walking down Barton's street at half-past ten? That's what we want to know."

Smithson father glared at Smithson son with such ferocity that even the latter realized he had said the wrong thing.

Dickie laughed.

"How do you know we were there? We never said so."

"Oh, Percy," Mary said, "you naughty boy! You must have been out in the dark by yourself. What *were* you doing? Did your mummy and daddy know?"

"If you really want to know," the tormented Percy

snarled, "I was posting a letter. But what were you doing there? That's what you've got to tell us."

Then pandemonium broke loose. Mr Smithson turned on Percy, who began to shout with rage. Mackie once again wriggled out of Mary's arms and, barking furiously, leaped joyfully for Percy, who tried to kick him. Mary ran forward to rescue the dog and Dickie put his head down and butted Mr Smithson hard in his soft middle as the latter made a grab at Mary.

And while this was going on there came a thunderous knocking on the door of the caravan, which was suddenly opened from outside.

The silence that followed was broken by Mary, who grabbed Mackie again and ran to the door.

"It's David!" she shouted. "And Tom too. How wonderful of you, David. We're quite ready to go now. Come on, Dickie."

Mr Smithson then came to the open door and told them all that they were trespassing, and that if ever they came near him or his caravan again he would see that they would regret it. Then he slammed the door so violently that the caravan rocked.

"Nice chap that," Tom said, handing them raincoats. "Did he touch you kids? Are you both all right?"

"We're fine, brave rescuers," Mary said. "But first of all I think we should wait for a few minutes in the lane just to see if he follows us, 'cos he does want to know what we're doing and where we are, and then you can tell us how you found us."

"And thanks for bringing the macks," Dickie added.

David laughed. "That was Peter's idea; she's at H.Q.2 making something hot for you." Then he explained how they had heard Mackie bark when they were in the wood, and as it began to rain hard they thought it wise to send out a rescue-party. By following the lane as the twins had done, they soon saw the lights of the caravan.

They waited briefly in the lane but were not followed, and twenty minutes later splashed through the puddles in the farmyard and slipped through the big doors of H.Q.2.

"Off with those shoes and socks," Peter said as she seized a twin in each hand. "Here's a towel to dry yourselves. Sit by the stove and here's some hot soup, and while you're having that you can tell me what's happened."

"Peter darling, you're just wonderful," Mary said as she kneeled thankfully by the stove.

But while she was sipping the soup she began to nod, and although she managed to say, "Come to think of it, we're sure dear Percy was taking a message somewhere. He acksherly *said* he'd gone to post a letter. I b'lieve he went to the post office all right, but I reckon he took a note for Mr Wilkins . . . Oh dear, Peter, I'm awfully sorry, but I don't think I can finish this, I'm too tired," she slipped sideways as her mug clattered on the floor.

Peter kneeled beside her.

"Help me up the stairs with her, David, and I'll put her to bed . . . Look, Tom! Dickie's going off too."

For many weeks after it was easy to torment the twins by reminding them that they could not possibly deny that they had both been put to bed that night.

7. Greystone Dingle

PETER WAS FIRST awake next morning and she was conscious of the steady, relentless drumming of the rain on the roof of the barn above her. She stretched luxuriously in her cosy sleeping-bag and turned over to look out of her window, but the light was grey and the glass so splashed with beating rain that she could see little.

It was raining as only it can rain in the hill country at the end of the summer. The sky was full of rain, and without looking further Peter knew that the clouds were shrouding the hill-tops and that just as the water was now gurgling in the gutters a few feet away, so it was running down the valleys and dingles of the Long Mynd and the Stiperstones.

After a while she yawned, kneeled up in her sleeping-bag and pressed her face against the window, realizing that the rain had stopped. She raised her hand and wiped away the mist of her breath from the glass and looked out. Someone was struggling up the hill between the trees. Whoever it was seemed to be in great distress, for while Peter watched the visitor slipped and fell in the muddy water twice before reaching the gate.

Suddenly Peter realized that it was Jenny—white-faced, bedraggled, stumbling in her heavy rubber boots.

Peter slipped out of her sleeping-bag, reached for her raincoat which she flung over her pyjamas, and ran for the stairs.

"Wake up, you lazy louts!" she shouted as she climbed down. "Wake up, David! . . . Jenny is outside, and she looks as if she's run all the way . . . Tom! *Wake up!* Jen's in trouble and it's late . . . Get up and give a hand."

Then came a desperate tattoo of blows on the great doors and a thin and breathless little voice pleading:

86

"Hurry! Hurry! Let me in! It's Jenny . . ."

"Don't worry, Jen," Peter shouted as she slipped back the bolt, "we're all here. Take it easy."

A gust of wind swirled into the great barn as Jenny stepped forward and grabbed Peter by the shoulders. She was sobbing and fighting for breath.

"Why, Jenny, what's wrong? Come and sit down and tell us all about it."

Jenny looked round wildly, gulped and tried to pull herself together as Tom ran forward and closed the door. Then David appeared and somehow they got her into a chair by the stove, where she collapsed and hid her face in her hands.

"Get the fire going, David," Peter snapped. "It ought to have been alight an hour ago . . . Tom! Pull her boots off and let's try and get her out of these wet things . . . Now, Jen, tell us what's happened."

Jenny shook her red curls back, sniffed and then smiled feebly.

"I'm sorry," she gasped. "Sorry to be such an idiot . . . He's gone!"

"Who's gone, Jen? What do you mean?" Tom asked as he passed a bundle of dry sticks to David.

"He has. Mr Wilkins . . . He went afore any of us were up."

"He'll come back," David said as he cupped a lighted match between his hands. "Don't worry, Jen."

"But I *do* worry, David. I've never worried about anything so much before. I've never been so unhappy in my whole life. Don't you see that you all trusted me to look after him, but I've failed you all and let him go."

"Don't talk nonsense, Jen," Tom said stoutly. "If the old chump has gone he's gone, and that's all there is to it . . . Anyway, I reckon that David is right and that he'll come back."

"But you all *trusted* me," Jenny wailed. "I found him for you, and this adventure was going to be mine for us all . . . I ought to have slept across his threshold and guarded him," she added dramatically. "I've *betrayed* you and the Club and I'll never forgive myself."

They did their best to comfort her, and while the boys went into their cubicles to dress they kept up a running fire of cross-talk with her until she had to laugh. Peter, after she had dressed, busied herself at the stove and said that they could not or would not do anything else until they had had breakfast. Dickie woke resentfully at last and complained about the noise, while Mary, who had quietly joined the group round the stove, smiled at Jenny.

"Don't you worry, Jen," she whispered. "Don't take any notice of what David says if you don't like what he's saying. We never do. It makes him mad, but it makes us much happier . . . Tell us all about it at breakfast."

The rain was pouring down again when they sat round the table twenty minutes later.

"Now then," Dickie said as he started on his porridge, "tell us, Jen. I want to know why you woke me up in that rude way just now."

"He slipped out of the house while we were all still in bed. He must have done. I've been puzzling to think why he should, because I'm sure he was happy, and I'd told him that we were all coming today to look after him . . . Do you think he's been kidnapped by those awful people? I'll never, never forgive myself . . ."

"Never mind about forgiving yourself," Tom said brutally. "Did he leave any message? Surely he wouldn't run off without explaining to Mrs Harman."

"That's just exactly what I was going to tell you next, Tom Ingles," Jenny replied with her nose in the air. "But I can't tell you if you keep interrupting. As it happens, he *did* leave a message addressed to Mum, and after she'd read it I slipped it into my pocket. I'm sure he wouldn't mind really, but I felt awful about it. It's because I've got this key to the mystery that I ran all the way here . . . This is it. Mum found it on the kitchen mantelpiece. Mr Wilkins must have gone out of the back door, because it had been unlocked, and when we looked in his room his haversack thing had gone and so had his bicycle. *Don't do that, Mary! It hurts!*"

Mary spoke with her mouth full.

"I pinched you a'purpose, Jenny . . . PLEASE read the letter."

"I think you're all mean. You might let me tell everything that happened properly. It's happened to me and Mr Wilkins and not to any of you . . . Oh! very well." And she unfolded the paper.

"MY DEAR MRS HARMAN,

With this you will find a week's board and lodging as arranged between us. Circumstances have arisen which make me believe that it would be better for all concerned if I left you at once. You must forgive the abrupt manner of my going and I ask you to accept my apologies for any inconvenience caused, but I am confident there will be trouble for you all if I stay with you.

Will you please convey my warm greetings to your daughter and thank her for befriending an old man. Tell her, if you please, to take the greatest care of her silver spoon, and that if she and her young friends wish to continue with their plan, I suggest that the dingle where we met yesterday—it is, I believe, called Greystone Dingle on the map—might be worth attention.

Again my thanks for kindness shown and my apologies for leaving you with such apparent lack of courtesy.

Yours truly,

GEORGE WILKINS.

P.S.—Should any letters come for me, please hold them until I call or write, and do not deliver them to anyone else without my authorization."

There was a long pause while Jenny folded up the letter and replaced it in her pocket. Then:

"So his name is George," Dickie said irrelevantly. "How peculiar."

"I don't see anything peculiar about it," Jenny said indignantly.

"That postscript sounds as if he intends to come back some time, anyway," David remarked. "But what do we do now?"

"Push all these dirty dishes in a bucket of water, clear up a bit and make a plan," Tom said briskly. "I vote we try and find old George."

"So do I," Jenny agreed. "But what was it that scared him so much that he rushed off like that without saying good-bye to me?"

Dickie jumped up from the table and, in spite of Peter's protests, began to toss the mugs and plates into the bucket of drinking water.

"Don't fuss, Peter," he begged. "Let's get on and *do* something more important than washing-up . . . *We* know what's happened, don't we, Mary?"

"Easy!" his twin replied. "When we saw young Percy last night he had been delivering a note from his father. I 'spect it would be an awful threatenin' letter . . . Blackmail, p'raps . . . When we asked him what he'd been doing he said he'd been to post a letter. I think he was terrified of us and let that out."

David pounced on the weakness of this argument by asking how Mr Wilkins could have found the note without the knowledge of anyone else in the house.

"But I didn't *ask* Mum or Dad whether a note had come for him last night," Jenny said. "I never thought of it."

"I suppose it doesn't matter very much, anyway," David said. "The point is that he's gone, and I think the twins are right when they say he was frightened away. Somehow or other the charming Smithsons must have convinced him that he would be less trouble to everybody if he joined with them and had nothing to do with us."

Peter agreed. "But he does send us a message," she pointed out. "He does suggest we explore Greystone Dingle. He wouldn't have said that if he hadn't meant something. Let's go there as soon as we can and explore."

Mary ran down the barn and flung back the doors. "That's what we've been trying to tell you ever since yesterday. We *must* go there. Dickie and me found a camping place . . . And look! The rain has stopped, and even if it pours we can shelter in the cave. Come on! Let's go!"

"Right!" David said. "Let's pack up as quickly as we can and get going. Everything we need on the trailer again and I'll remind you all that we've got a long way to go. If there's any Roman treasure to be found, and old man Wilkins thinks it's in Greystone Dingle, we may as well camp there as anywhere else—but on our way I think it would be a good idea to see whether the Smithsons have moved their camp."

Tom turned to David.

"Could you manage the trailer if Jen and I went on ahead? I reckon if we went off quickly now we'd have more chance of tracing the Smithsons and old Wilkins . . . Will you leave that to us? Maybe we'll pick you up somewhere on the road, but if we all keep together we shall be very slow . . . Besides, if Jen is going to camp with us she'll want to let them know at home and get her stuff together, and we can call in there on our way after we've checked up on the Smithsons. What do you think?"

"It's a good enough scheme, but I don't see how we'll get the trailer down the hill without you."

"We think it would be a good idea if Mary and me went on ahead to the camping place and staked a claim," Dickie said, "but we don't suppose any of you will think that's a good idea."

"You're right again, Dickie," Peter said. "We'll risk someone else getting there first, but you needn't think that David and I are going to pack the trailer and struggle up and down hill with it by ourselves. We're on a holiday too. . . . Anyway, here comes Charles. I know he'll help us down with it, and I think Tom and Jenny should go now. That really is a brainwave."

So as Charles splashed towards them through the puddles in the farmyard, Tom pulled Jenny to her feet.

"Come on, Jenny, let's not waste time talking. We've got a lot to do . . . Good morning, Charles, and cheerio, too. The others will give you all the news," and almost before poor Jenny had got her breath he had grabbed her old mack in one hand and her arm in the other, and was leading her across the farmyard.

"Oh, Tom," she gasped, "I know I'll enjoy this adventure very much just with you, but do you really think it's fair to the others?"

Tom turned at the white gate and called back:

"Meet you at the camp site in Greystone if we don't see you before. Good luck!" Then to Jenny: "They'll manage, Jen."

Ten minutes later they were in Barton, and then Tom led her down the narrow passage between the houses into the lane where David and he had come last night to find the twins.

"I suppose the caravan was in Higgins's field, then," Jenny said. "There's another way out of it, of course. They couldn't get the car through here, but it would be a short-cut for Percy."

She ran ahead and peered through a gap in the hedge. "They're not there now, although there's a pile of rubbish in the corner of the field. Litter louts!"

Tom insisted that they should go over and examine the Smithsons' litter just in case they had left a clue. There were empty broken bottles, old tins, a chocolate box, three newspapers, cigarette packets and some pieces of a torn-up letter.

"I wonder if we ought to collect those bits and try and put 'em together," Tom said as he stirred them with his foot. "I reckon that's what a detective would do."

Jenny's voice shook with excitement. "Do it, then. Let's do it," and she went down on her knees and began to pick up the pieces.

As soon as they began to fit the little squares together it was obvious that there were only a few words of hand-writing to decipher.

"Somebody began a letter and didn't finish it," he said. "I do that when it's going to be difficult. I mean I have one or two shots at it first . . ."

Then he cocked his head on one side and read: " '*You know we can make trouble for you. You know we can find you wherever you go, so why don't you behave sensible?*' That's all it says, Jen."

"It's enough, isn't it?" she replied sensibly. "Come on, Tom. Let's get home and see if Dad knows anything about the note which Percy did bring."

Mr Harman looked gravely at his daughter when the bell over the door clanged and announced their arrival.

"Morning, Tom . . . Now, my girl, where have you been, and why did you dash off like a lunatic without your breakfast?"

Jenny slipped round the counter. "*Please* don't be cross with me, Dad! I *had* to go and tell the others that Mr Wilkins had disappeared because, you see, I had promised to look after him. But the most important thing now, Dad, is this. Do you know if anybody brought him a note last night?"

Mr Harman looked surprised.

"Certainly he had a note delivered here last night," he admitted. "A pimply boy banged on the door and brought it while you were up at Seven Gates. I took it upstairs to him myself . . . But what's that got to do with you rushing off this morning?"

Jenny tried to explain once again, and Tom put in a word when he could and made it clear that Jenny was expected to come camping with them now and that they must be on their way just as soon as she could get everything packed up.

"This isn't camping weather, Tom. It will be raining again in an hour . . . Seems to me you youngsters are all crazy."

They explained that they had everything in the trailer which they needed for a camp, and that they had found a cave in Greystone Dingle.

93

At last Jenny got permission and before either Mr or Mrs Harman could change their minds she gathered a few things into a rucksack and rejoined Tom.

On their way down the street she stopped once or twice to ask neighbours if they had seen the Smithsons' car and caravan in the early morning, but nobody could give them any news of the strangers.

The sun had broken through the clouds now, and, as the wind had dropped, it was very sultry as they trudged along the road with the bulk of the great hill on their right and the blue-green of the wood before them.

"Maybe we've been rather mean in going off on our own," Tom said. "I never thought of it like that before, but it won't be much fun hauling that trailer all the way here . . . When we get to the track through the trees where we saw them yesterday we'll have a rest before exploring the dingle. It's just round the next corner, I reckon."

But Tom did not get the rest for, five minutes later, when they stepped thankfully off the road on to a soft carpet of pine needles, they heard voices just ahead.

Jenny grabbed Tom's arm and hissed:

"That's them. I'm sure it is. It's that horrible boy. Listen, Tom."

Although they strained they could not hear the words spoken in a man's voice, but Percy's reply was clear enough.

"I can't help it. I can't move the car, so you can't come this way, and that's all there is to it. I don't think my father would like people like you here, so you'd better go away before he comes back . . ."

Jenny grabbed Tom's hand and pulled him forward.

"We *must* see who it is. Come on! I think that boy is the vilest I've ever known."

They crept forward between the trees, and then Tom heard Jenny draw in her breath sharply.

"It's Reuben," she whispered. "Reuben and Miranda, our gipsy friends!"

A few yards ahead, where the rough track narrowed but

94

was still just wide enough for a car to pass through, they saw the back of a gaily-painted and familiar caravan. The way into the dingle was blocked by an equally familiar car and luxurious caravan, and there was not even room between the tree-trunks for the gipsies' van to be turned.

"Just a sec, Jen," Tom whispered. "Don't let them see you yet. Listen!"

The slow, lilting voice of the man came to them clearly now.

"But can you not see, boy, that I can move neither forward nor back? If your father is not far away perhaps you would ask him to kindly move his car so that I can drive through."

"What?" replied the gentlemanly Percy, "me leave the car with you here? Not likely. I'm staying here just to see that people like you don't come and pinch anything. If you want to wait to see my dad I can't stop you, but I don't suppose you'll like it much when he does come."

Before the gipsy could answer, Jenny shook off Tom's restraining hand and dashed forward.

"Hello, Reuben," she called. "Hello, Miranda—and Fenella, too! How wonderful to see you again. Do you remember us?"

The olive-skinned woman with a coloured scarf over her head turned with a smile of welcome at the sound of Jenny's voice.

"Jenny! Jenny Harman. To be sure I remember."

"Where are you going, Reuben? The others will hate to miss you," said Jenny.

"We have an old camping ground in this dingle, my little dear," the gipsy answered. "We shall be here perhaps for two or three days . . . And the others? Petronella and the twins? Where are they?"

Suddenly Jenny remembered that they were not alone. Percy, standing guard by his father's car, was gazing at them all in open-mouthed astonishment. At the gipsies' reference to "the others," he looked a little more intelligent

95

and then caught Tom's eye and retreated a few steps.

"Don't you dare touch me," he muttered. "If you come near me I'll press the horn of the car and my father will come."

"He's near enough for that, is he?" Tom said with a grin. "Press the horn, then, and fetch your father so that he can move and let our friends through. You've no right to park your car right there. Why don't you leave it off the road, where it belongs?"

"Friends!" Percy sneered. "They can't be your friends. They're gipsies!"

Miranda flushed at this and grabbed her daughter Fenella, who was often too shy to speak, by the hand. But before she could answer, Jenny whispered:

"*Please* come away from this horrible boy and I'll tell you everything and why we're here. I'm sure he won't move, so please persuade Reuben to come back to the road —just to the edge of the wood, where we can talk."

Miranda spoke quickly in Romany to her husband, who shrugged his shoulders and went to the horse's head.

"We cannot turn here, so we go backwards," he smiled. Slowly and skilfully he backed the horse and van down the sandy track, while Tom, who was helping him, looked back over his shoulder and called to Percy, who was now nibbling his finger-nails.

"Don't fret, my lad. We'll come back for you later."

As soon as there was room between the trees they turned the caravan and Jenny whispered to Tom, "Even if we haven't found Mr Wilkins we do know that the Smithsons are somewhere up the dingle . . . By what he said they can hardly be anywhere else, can they, Tom? I think we'll have to warn the others now, because unless Mr Smithson moves his car I don't see how we'll get the trailer past . . . Of course, you and me can just walk past Percy, but I think David would like to know what we've found."

"And I bet he'd like some help with the trailer too," Tom grinned. "Anyway, let's talk to Reuben now and tell him the others are on their way. I wish you'd show them your spoon, Jen."

The gipsy, now whistling cheerfully, led the horse to the grass verge at the side of the road, flung the reins over its back and said, "Now tell us why you are here and what you know about the boy who speaks so big."

"We're the advance guard for the whole Lone Pine army really," said Jenny. "But I thought you hated all the country by the Stiperstones and the Devil's Chair and never came anywhere near if you could help it."

"This dingle is different," Miranda explained. "Greystone it is called, but it is not like the other dingles, for it is cleansed by running water."

"Oh!" Jenny said vaguely. "Thank you very much for telling me. I see." But really she didn't.

Tom and Jenny then told a combined and rather confused story. Neither Reuben nor Miranda seemed to be very interested in Mr Wilkins, but when Jenny at last tugged at the hidden ribbon round her neck and produced the silver spoon, they both examined it carefully.

"He—Mr Wilkins, I mean—says the Romans made this spoon and that it's worth a lot of money. And he says that the Romans lived up in these hills and mined lead and that if we could find where they built their houses then we might discover some more of the things they made, and that people in museums will buy these things the Romans made, if you see what I mean, Reuben and Miranda. What do you think?"

Reuben relit his pipe. "I think the spoon is real," he said as he got up, "although we know nothing of the worth of these things. I will show you something that we found in this very dingle not many years ago."

When he came back and opened his clenched hand they saw what looked to be two tiny buttons of dirty metal.

"You may touch them," he said to Jenny, "but take care, for they are easily lost, and a learned man told me once that these are Roman money . . . Look closely and you will see faint markings of a head as on our coins today."

"Are they gold?" Jenny gasped.

"Bronze, I was told. I have others and so have other Romany, and most have been found in these hills."

"And you found these in Greystone Dingle, Reuben? Right here? Near here, I mean?"

"I could show you where, Tom. 'Twas right by the stream. I could sell them, but I like to keep them."

Suddenly Jenny jumped to her feet and dashed round the caravan into the wood.

"Quick, Tom! Catch him! That was Percy spying on us. The dirty little sneak was listening to everything we were saying."

They started after him and then Tom stopped suddenly.

"No need to chase him, Jenny. If you're sure it was him, that's good enough. We know where he is, and somehow I don't think he'll move. Let's go and meet the others, give 'em a hand with the trailer and decide how we're going to get into the dingle . . . I reckon we'll have plenty of time and opportunities for dealing with Master Percy."

When they got back to the caravan Reuben was climbing up to the driving seat.

"We go on beyond Barton to camp," he said. "No need to stay here and make trouble. Everybody is always ready to blame the Romany if there is trouble, and we do not like that boy, and neither do we think we should like his father."

"If you're going into Barton you'll meet the others soon, Reuben. May we come with you some of the way?" Jenny asked, and when he smiled and nodded she added, "*Please* may I drive the caravan? I'll be very, very careful, I promise."

So Reuben got down again and went to the horse's head, and Jenny, with Miranda on one side and Fenella on the other, took the reins in her hands while Tom walked at the side. And so they met David, Peter, the twins and Mackie a mile out of Barton Beach, and it was not a very happy meeting. Both David and Peter, who were pulling the heavily-loaded trailer, were very hot and bad tempered.

Peter was the first to see the caravan coming towards them and Jenny noticed that she said something to David, pointed ahead and then stopped. Tom shouted and waved and Jenny just shouted, but no answering hail of welcome came from the Lone Piners.

"I think you'd better drive now, Miranda," Jenny said hastily. "I think I'll get down and explain. They don't seem very pleased to see us."

"Well, well," David said as Jenny and Tom came up to them about twenty yards ahead of the caravan, "how nice! We do hope you're enjoying yourselves and having a really nice ride while we pull this lovely trailer up and down hills."

"I suppose Tom rides as soon as he gets tired," Peter added. "That's nice for him, too. I suggested a ride for myself on the trailer just now, but David didn't think much of the idea."

Tom flushed with annoyance and then laughed.

"Idiots!" he said. "We're sorry if the trailer is a nuisance, but we came back to help you. We've found Percy and the Smithsons, anyway, and we've lots of news."

But Jenny was angry. She hated her friend Peter to talk like that.

"However bad tempered you *feel*," she said, "you might at least speak decently to Reuben and Miranda and Fenella. We met them in the wood and we came back together to meet you."

Then David grinned sheepishly and Peter laughed and said, "Sorry," while the twins and Mackie ran to meet the gipsies. But they did not stay very long, for Reuben was anxious to get on, and when David and Peter had heard the others' story they were more certain than ever that they should be in the dingle as soon as possible.

"But you won't be able to get past their beastly car," Jenny said. "Reuben couldn't get the caravan by, and although the trailer isn't as big the trees are in the way. He's put his car there on purpose and left Percy on guard."

"We'll see about that," David said grimly. "Somehow I don't think little Percy will stop me."

"Let's harness him to the trailer," Dickie said, "and make him pull it by himself."

"A beast of burden," Mary murmured. "Specially the beast. Gorgeous!"

It was not long before they reached the edge of the wood again. On the way Tom told David everything that had happened once more, and it was agreed that, although they had not yet found Mr Wilkins, it was first of all important to establish their camp and to see what the Smithsons were doing in the dingle.

At the end of the track David stopped and said: "We're going to get past the Smithsons' car if it's still parked there. I've got two axes in the trailer, and we'll cut down one or two trees if they're not too big. Tom says that young Percy threatened to warn his father by sounding the horn of the car, so if he's still there I think he ought to be prevented from doing that. I'd like to surprise Mr Smithson wherever he is. Who'll look after Percy?"

"We will," Dickie said promptly. "We'll see to him. He's terrified of us, anyway, and we promise he won't sound the warning."

"We'll creep on ahead like Indians on the trail," Mary said, "and get round behind him . . . Come on, Dickie!" and with Mackie they slipped like shadows between the tree-trunks and disappeared.

"They'll manage that job," Peter laughed. "This is going to be fun. Come on!"

They hauled the trailer over the pine needles and were quite close to the parked car and caravan before Percy saw them. At first he looked scared, but when Peter said, "Is your father far away? Will you ask him to move the car, please, so that we can get by?" he replied with all his usual charm. "Why do you want to get by with all that old rubbish? I can't move the car, so you can't get by. You'd better go back."

David, who had been examining the trees and making

up his mind that only two small larches need be cut down, turned to Tom, who passed him one of the axes just as Jenny said:

"Do *please* tell us if you have seen dear old Mr Wilkins. We've lost him and we're very worried. I know you and your parents are friendly with him, and we wondered if you knew where he was."

"Wouldn't yer like ter know!" Percy sneered. "I'll bet anything you want to know where he is, but you ain't going to know . . . Now you'd better get out. You can't get by, so you'd better go before my dad gets after yer."

David, with the axe behind his back, watched him carefully. He certainly looked very smug and sure of himself. It might be that he knew something. Out of the corner of his eye David then noticed the twins on the far side of the car, and was pleased to see that Percy was not expecting an attack from the rear. He brought the axe from behind his back, raised it by both hands above his shoulders, and dealt a terrific, perfectly timed blow at the base of the first tree.

" 'Ere!" Percy yelled, "yer can't do that." And then made the mistake of advancing a few steps. David struck again just as Tom, with the other axe, lashed out at the other tree which was barring their way.

David laughed. "But we *can* do it . . . Stand back if you don't want to be hurt, and notice that you won't be able to sound the horn on that car to warn your father . . . You stay quiet, little man, and nobody will hurt you for the moment . . . Just see that he doesn't run away, Peter. Jenny will help you if you need any."

The two girls closed in on Percy, and when he turned round the twins were standing in front of the closed door of the car and smiling at him sweetly. He was trapped and helpless and knew it.

Five minutes later the two trees were down and the trailer had been hauled out into the open.

"Do you give me your word that you won't move from here, little rat?" David said. "We'd hate to tie you and gag you, but I suppose that if you do promise you'll break it if it suits you. What are you going to do?"

"I'll keep quiet," Percy sulked. "Dirty bullies, all of you! Six of you to one . . ."

Farther up the track they were warned by the clink of metal on stone and the sound of Smithson's voice. David held up his hand and the trailer stopped. Then, with Peter, he tiptoed forward until they could see round a pile of loose rocks at a sharp turn in the track.

Round the corner the track, which looked as if it had once been the bed of a stream, widened, and here, digging rather feebly among the loose stones, was Mr Wilkins. A few yards away Mr Smithson, with his hands on his hips and a cigar in his mouth, was watching him, and a little farther off Mrs Smithson was sitting on a rock smoking a cigarette.

"The beasts!" Peter whispered. "They're making him do it. What shall we do?"

David pulled her back round the rocks and spoke to the twins.

"How much farther to the camping place?"

"Not far," Dickie said confidently. "I remember this. 'Bout two more turns and we're there . . . Is it them? Mr Wilkins, too?"

Peter told them what they had seen and then David made his decision. "I'm sure we must go ahead and make camp. When we've got our headquarters we can leave a sentry and explore. We must get the trailer past, and I suggest we don't take any notice of any of them, and that includes Mr Wilkins, Jenny. Let's all pretend we don't know him, and I guess that will confuse Smithson a bit. He won't know what to believe."

It was very difficult for Jenny to obey these orders, but Mr Wilkins made it easier for them, for, after a quick smile of recognition as they came talking and laughing round the corner, he, too, pretended not to know them as Smithson let out a bellow of rage.

" 'Ere!" he shouted as David brushed by him hauling

the trailer, "what are you kids doing? And 'ow did yer get in 'ere, I'd like to know? I left the car in the path."

Mrs Smithson jumped to her feet.

"Percy!" she shouted. "What have you done to my Percy? . . . Oh dear! Oh dear! Maybe they've kidnapped him!" She turned and stumbling among the stones disappeared round the corner.

"Excuse me, sir," David said politely, "but will you please move? You know quite well you daren't stop us and we've a perfect right to be here . . . We're camping in the hills."

Sullenly Mr Smithson moved aside and the Lone Pine procession moved with dignity up the dingle. Not one of them looked back.

8. Powerless Percy

It was after six when Dickie woke the next morning. Although he was very snug in his sleeping-bag it was a moment or two before he remembered where he was. Then he turned on his back and saw a ceiling of rock above him and realized that he was in the cave in Greystone Dingle. He remembered that the Lone Piners had now established themselves in H.Q.4 and that today there would almost certainly be some fun.

The morning smelled fresh and clean, and when he sat up he saw that it was no longer raining and that the red, watery sun was doing its best to dispel the mist. A yard away on his right Mary was still sleeping, and he could hear Peter and Jenny breathing gently in the gloom at the back of the cave. Outside, on the little plateau perched above the dingle, was the tent in which David and Tom were apparently still sleeping.

It seemed a pity to waste a beautiful morning, Dickie thought. Perhaps there was something that could be done before the others woke? Suddenly he realized what that something ought to be, wriggled out of his bag and scrambled into his jeans and sweater. Then he tiptoed across to his twin, kneeled down beside her, and with his mouth to her ear whispered, "Wake up, Mary. I've got an idea for us . . . Come out *quietly* when you are ready and don't wake the others."

She was with him in three minutes, and together they crept past the tent and down the little track which took them to the dingle. Mackie trotted happily at their heels.

As soon as they were out of earshot, Dickie said, "Do you know what it is, twin? Do you know what we ought to be doing right now?"

"Yes, I do. We ought to be getting sticks for the fire, 'cos we're the first to wake, and I s'pose we ought to be lugging a pail of water up to the cave, too."

He snorted with disgust. "Just like a girl! . . . There's plenty of people there to do that sort of thing, but what I want us to do is to go down right now and see if we can rescue Mr Wilkins."

"Dickie! That's a marvellous idea, but how can we do it . . . I mean, where is he and what shall we do with him when we've got him?"

"I don't think you're properly awake, twin," Dickie said. "I'm disappointed with you this morning, 'cos you keep on saying stupid things. It doesn't really matter what we do with him, does it? We can just give him to Jenny."

Mary nodded. "Sorry, Dickie . . . Let's go and spy on them. I'd better carry Mackie in case he barks . . ."

The nearer they got to the wood and the road where the Smithsons had left their caravan, the thicker was the mist, and they shivered in the damp chill.

"We shall be able to get close to their camp if it's still in the same place," Mary whispered through chattering teeth. "Careful, Dickie. We must be nearly there."

The fog hid them as they tiptoed across the wet grass between the foot of the dingle and the wood, but they did not realize how close they were to the caravan until a puff of wind sighed through the trees and began to move the mist. Then the sun tried a little harder and they both turned and ran back to the shelter of a gorse bush as the shapes of car, caravan and two tents became clear.

Dickie was curious.

"If old man Wilkins is in one of those tents I could creep up and tell him we're here and that he's only got to come with us and be rescued."

Mary was dubious. "Sounds too easy, twin. It won't happen like that . . . *LOOK!* I think someone is moving in that near tent . . . Anyway, Dickie, if he really is their prisoner, they'd lock him in the caravan . . . *Yes, it is.* Someone's coming out . . . *Quiet, Mackie.*"

As they crouched behind the gorse bush, speechless with excitement, the flaps of the little tent nearest to them shook, and then, rather like something emerging from a chrysalis, Percy, fully dressed, crawled out into the daylight. The boy stretched, rubbed his tousled head and yawned. Then he strolled over to the caravan. It was difficult for the two spies to see exactly what he did because the tents were in the way, but it seemed as if he was peering through the window in the door.

"What shall we do now, Mary?" Dickie whispered.

"Did you say what shall we do?" Mary returned.

Dickie nodded, and then they looked at each other and, without words, began to giggle.

Then followed the seduction of Percy.

As he crossed the little clearing towards his tent Mary stood up, moved from behind the gorse bush and waved to him. As he stopped short in surprise she put her finger to her lips and beckoned. She stood there with the morning mist glinting on her curls. She looked very shy and afraid. Her violet eyes—always attractively large—were now dewy with unshed tears, and her lower lip trembled a little as she beckoned the reluctant Percy and whispered, "*Please* come over and help us . . . We've come all this way to find you . . . Do *please* come."

Slowly and suspiciously he advanced towards the bush, while Dickie quietened Macbeth.

"What you kids doing here?" Percy said as soon as he was in earshot. "You'd better get out quick before I wake my father . . . And keep that dog away."

"We've come to ask you to help us," Mary whispered. "But it's a secret and we don't want any of the grown-ups to know . . . We did so hope you would be awake, Percy . . . I was just telling you that we—that's my twin and me—are sure you're the only one who can help us. Will you come up the dingle a little way so that we can tell you everything? . . . *Please*, Percy."

Slowly the twins led their victim away, but when they were round the bend of the dingle and could no longer see the caravan, he stopped short and said suspiciously:

"What's the game, anyway. What do you two kids want?"

Shamelessly they flattered him and asked his advice. Shamelessly they betrayed their friends by telling him how badly they were treated by the other Lone Piners.

"It's because we're smaller than they are," Mary said bravely, but with a sob in her throat. "We're the youngest, you see, and they're big and they're too busy for us. They're stronger, too."

"And they bully us," Dickie gulped.

"What's all this got to do with me anyway?" Percy inquired with some logic.

"Well, you see, Percy" (this was Mary, of course), "we did rather hope that maybe you'd sort of join up with us and help us to show the grown-ups and these stuck-up, bossy seniors how clever we are . . . Would you, Percy? We know a few things about this adventure."

Percy tried to look cunning, but only succeeded in looking meaner than usual. "What adventure? Is it to do with that red-haired kid what lives in Barton?"

Mary thought that it might be better to evade a direct answer to this question, but that it would be safe to say, "Oh! Jenny Harman, you mean? We can't stand her. We hate her, don't we, Dickie?"

"We do. She's almost the worse, except David and Tom. But it was exciting when Tom found that you-know-what and gave it to her, wasn't it, twin? I s'pose that really started everything, didn't it?"

"I wish you'd explain what you're talking about," Percy snapped. "What do you mean? You just tell me what he gave that red-head that started everything . . . And hurry, because I want my breakfast."

Then they launched into a long, complicated and entirely imaginary story about something which Tom had found when he was at work on the farm. They contradicted each other, they flattered Percy unceasingly, they sneered at Tom and Jenny and when their victim asked a question they got him and themselves into such a muddle with evasive answers that all three of them lost touch with the original question. But they got Percy into a good humour and kept him guessing until they had passed the little plateau of H.Q.4 and were scrambling up the narrowing, stony track towards the top of the Stiperstones. Then, very subtly, Dickie changed the tone of the conversation, just when Percy was becoming really condescending. They told him legends of the Stiperstones and the Devil's Chair, and showed him how the latter was now hidden in mist and what this meant. They recounted with gusto all the eerie legends they had ever heard of this strange countryside, and many more besides. It was Mary who first noticed that their victim's sallow face became paler still and that his voice shook with fear as he questioned them. Just for a moment she felt sorry for him, for he was really frightened, but then she caught Dickie's eye and her heart was hardened.

They were passing a narrow, lonely cleft in the rocky hillside when Dickie stepped in front of Percy and nodded to his twin. Then they fell upon him. Dickie turned and hurled himself at the victim's knees and brought him down, while Mary, like a little fury, flung herself at him from behind.

They rolled him on to his face and forced his arms behind his back. Mary, sobbing with fury and muttering, "You beastly little beast! You didn't really think we *liked* you, did you? We'll teach you to throw rocks at little dogs," sat on his head and helped her twin to tie his hands together with his tie. Then Dickie rolled him back again, and as Percy began to kick out furiously they each fell upon a leg and tied his shoe laces together while he raged and fumed.

"Let me go," their victim snivelled.

"We told you that nobody could do what you did to this dog and not be sorry," said Mary. "Now you're going to have lots of time to be sorry up here with the old Devil who is sitting on his throne now . . . I s'pect we'll let you starve to death . . . Sorry, Mackie, but you've got to stay and guard him . . . Come on, Dickie."

Even when they were round the next corner they could still hear Percy's cries for help.

Dickie looked at Mary uneasily.

"We're not really bullyin' him, are we, twin? O' course, I know it serves him right, but . . ."

"I know how you feel, twin, 'cos I feel the same. Maybe we were a bit rough, but he started it all, and he shouldn't throw stones at dogs and be cheeky to us . . . What are we going to do now?"

"Get some food and more odds and ends and then go back to torture him—or pretend to—until we find out something about Mr Wilkins and what he really is doing for them . . . If we don't go back now they'll all wake up and fuss and come and look for us and spoil everything . . . There they are. They've got up and the fire's going, and I only hope one of them has fetched the water . . . Come on, twin. Don't tell 'em a thing. I'll get round Peter for some food and we'll be off again as quickly as we can."

They climbed the track to the little plateau and smiled sweetly on David.

"Good morning, David . . . Hello, Tom . . ."

David stood up and Tom joined him, barring the way into the cave.

"Where have you two been?" he said. "How long have you been out, and who said you could go, anyway? You know perfectly well that everyone has to take a share in helping to run the camp."

"We've been out looking for things," Dickie said, truthfully enough. "Things to help you, maybe, but private things too . . ."

"Where's Mackie?" David said suspiciously.

"He's all right," Mary smiled. "Don't you worry about him . . . Hello, Peter and Jenny."

The four seniors stood round the twins in a silent circle—"One at each corner," as Dickie remarked later—but their disapproval failed to impress them. Mary looked at them curiously as if she had never seen them before and then gazed into the sky, which was clouding over again. Dickie thrust his hands in his pockets and whistled "Oh! What a beautiful morning!"

Jenny tried to stifle a giggle, and then Peter said: "What *have* you been up to? It wasn't fair to go off like that without leaving a note. We were worried."

"I wasn't," Tom snorted. "Put it on record that I'm never likely to worry about either of 'em. They're too young to be brought on a trip like this."

Mary put out her tongue at him as Dickie spoke to Peter.

"That's all right, Peter. Don't worry about us. As Tom thinks we're too young to be with you we'll go off by ourselves . . . Matter of fact, we've got a secret camp of our own, so if you'll just let us have our share of the food we'll be on our way."

"Don't give them any food, Peter," David said.

The twins then strolled out of the circle and Dickie went into the cave and began to pack some things in his rucksack while Mary stood on guard outside.

"So you're going to let us starve, are you, Peter?" she said sweetly. "Not even a biscuit for breakfast? Well, you'll all be sorry one day when the hawks and things up here have picked our bleached bones clean . . . Ready, twin? Let's go, then."

Dickie turned halfway down the track.

"If you should happen to want old Mr Wilkins, Jenny," he called, "just let us know—if you can find us! Just leave it all to us."

"You'd better not spoil everything we fixed for you all," Mary added. "Don't try and do anything today without us, else you'll be sorry . . . If we don't come back, thro' lack of nourishment, maybe Mackie will lead you to us."

"That's right," Dickie added. "Dogs last longer than twins without food." And then, unexpectedly, he raised his arm in salute and added, "Farewell!"

As soon as they were out of sight round the corner of the dingle Peter laughed.

"They're up to something. Let's have breakfast and then go and find them."

"Leave 'em alone, I say," Tom remarked. "They'll come back when they're hungry."

"I think you're all rather beastly to the twins," Jenny said stoutly. "I think it must be wonderful to be a twin. It's one of the things I've always wanted to be."

David pointed out that whatever she wanted to be was nothing to do with how the twins were behaving now. "But I do agree," he went on, "that they're really up to something. They were definitely smug . . ."

Half an hour later the four were sitting comfortably round the fire enjoying breakfast, while David, in his usual logical way, was arguing that although it was great fun to have a camp like this and enemies like the Smithsons, they still did not really know whether Mr Wilkins knew what he was talking about.

"Of *course* he does," Jenny protested. "You're most unfair to him, David. You always have been. Didn't we see him digging down the dingle yesterday? Anyway, I *know* that what he's told me is true. Haven't I got this?" and dramatically she whisked out the strange silver spoon from inside her jersey. "It's very precious and it really *is* Roman treasure, I'm sure."

"Is it?" said a strange voice. "Who said so?"

"Mr Wilkins, of course," Jenny said without thinking. And then, when she saw the expression of horror on Peter's face, she turned round and saw Mr and Mrs Smithson watching them from a few yards away.

"Show me that spoon," the man demanded.

With a scuffle and wriggle Jenny restored her treasure to its temporary resting-place and then stood up with the others and faced their enemies across the camp-fire.

There was a long silence, and then Smithson, with a horrid leer, took a step forward and held out his hand.

"Please let me see that bit of old metal, kid. Just for

a moment. I'm interested in things like that."

"I know," Jenny said. "That's what we're afraid of. I won't show it to you and I won't sell it for any money in the world . . . Where's Mr Wilkins?"

David looked at her with admiration and smiled when he saw Smithson's face. Somehow or other Jenny had got her courage back!

Mrs Smithson looked a wreck. Her stockings were torn, her dyed hair awry, and the make-up on her face was rather like a clown's. After a few uneasy moments she gulped and said, "Never mind about that now . . . Have any of you kids seen my Percy this morning?"

David smiled at the idea which suddenly occurred to him.

"Since you ask us so politely," he said cheerfully, "we have *not* seen Percy. Has he run away from you?"

"That's enough of your cheek," Smithson blustered, while Mrs Smithson plucked at her lip with a painted finger-nail and then turned on him.

"You see. I know what's happened. Percy told me yesterday that he'd had trouble with some dirty gipsies and sent 'em off packing . . . Now they've come back and kidnapped my precious out of his tent . . . That's what has happened . . . He told me about 'em."

"Then he's a liar," Peter said quietly. "Those gipsies aren't dirty and he didn't send them off packing, because we were there. The gipsies are real Romanies. They're clean and kind and friends of ours, and I know they wouldn't do any harm to anybody. They certainly wouldn't want Percy."

"They wouldn't get anything for him," Tom murmured to himself, and then Smithson, with a roar of rage, shouted:

"That's what you are, then—friends o' dirty gipsies, and I reckon you're in on this racket . . . You'll soon be in trouble if that's your game. Maybe the police would like to know about the spoon that girl has got tied round her neck. Stolen, like as not."

David stepped forward.

"That's not true," he said, "and you know you've no right to say it. That spoon was given to my friend here and we have not seen your son today, nor do we know where he is . . . Will you please go now?"

"Where's those twin brats?" the woman suddenly yelled. "And that dog too. Where are they, I'd like to know? There's something fishy going on here. Maybe they're hiding in that cave . . . Go in and look," she added to her husband.

David was determined not to let the Smithsons into the cave, but doubted whether he and Tom between them could stop the big bully. But he was saved from making a difficult decision by Jenny, who pointed down to the stony track and shouted, "Look who's here!"

Down the track, trotting sedately, came Macbeth.

"He's got something in his mouth," Peter laughed. *"Good boy, Mackie . . . Come here!"*

David dodged past Mr Smithson and ran down to meet the little dog, who wagged his tail in friendly recognition. Then he stooped and took a folded paper from Mackie's mouth. Two words showed up and he was certainly surprised when he read, "Mister Smithson." After patting the dog, David strolled up to the camp-fire.

"For you," he said as he passed over the message.

The Smithsons, who had come forward a few paces to meet David, took the paper as if it was impregnated with a poison, one touch of which meant death. As they unfolded it and began to read its message, David, out of the corner of his eye, saw Tom whisper something to Jenny, and then, very quietly, behind the Smithsons' backs, they both began to creep away from the fire towards the edge of the plateau. Meanwhile, Smithson's face turned a rich purple as he shouted:

"What is this nonsense? Where is my boy? This is no time for kids' silly jokes . . . ANSWER ME!"

His wife plucked at his sleeve and pointed down the valley, where Tom and Jenny were running, hand in hand, in the direction of his caravan.

"COME BACK, YOU TWO BRATS! . . . I'LL HAVE YOU FOR TRESPASS, I WILL!"

And then, with another roar of rage, he grabbed the arm of his unfortunate wife and, stumbling and tripping, began a hopeless chase down the stony track.

Peter began to laugh until the tears streamed down her face.

"That was marvellous, David. Look at them! She'll fall any moment now. She's got high heels. Maybe he'll desert her, but he'll never catch Tom and Jenny. What do you think they're going to do?"

David wiped his eyes.

"I don't know. See if old Wilkins is in their camp, I should think . . ."

Peter stooped and picked up the note which Smithson had dropped in his rage.

"It's from Dickie, I'm sure. I know his writing. Read it, David."

David read: "*Mister Smithson, dear sir. Percy is in our power. He is powerless Percy now. He has been dissiplined very much and is quite quiet and good now. If you want him back you must send our friend Mr Wilkins to come and fetch him. We will swop Percy for Mr Wilkins. You must hang a white flag in the window of your caravan and then send Mr Wilkins up the Dingle to us till he finds us. Never mind who we are who have got Percy. Just show the white flag like we demand.*"

"Nice work," David commented as he folded the paper and put it in his pocket. "They shall have breakfast now . . . and if I'm not mistaken, they're coming for it now. Look hard at that rock down there. I swear I saw Mary peep round it."

He was right. His sister suddenly stood up and yelled:

"All right, Dickie. All clear. Bring him in quick."

Then Dickie arose from hiding and ran forward, leading the captive Percy at the end of a rope. Poor Percy was a sorry sight. His hands were tied behind him, his lank hair was soaking wet, he was gagged with one of his own socks, and there was no fight left in him.

"He doesn't look worth Mr Wilkins," Peter said, "but they ought not to do that, you know, David."

"Quick, David," Dickie said out of the side of his mouth, "gimme a torch, quick. We'll keep this at the back of the cave where the rocks fell. We may have to tie it up, though it's fairly tame now."

Mary grinned wickedly at her seniors.

"Just leave it all to us. We'll manage everything for you. If Smithson comes back without Wilkins don't let him in, will you? Don't let him know we're here."

Before either Peter or David could answer there came a shout from the valley below and they turned to see Tom struggling up the hill towards them. He shouted something which they could not hear, so Peter ran down to meet him.

Tom stopped and struggled to find the breath to speak when he saw her coming, and when she asked, "Anything wrong, Tom? Jenny all right?" he could only gasp and shake his head.

At last, "Sorry, Peter . . . Ran all the way up hill . . . I've got news. Old Wilkins has gone. Just as we got in sight of the caravan we saw him break the door down and run off into the wood. Jen has gone after him, but we thought you ought to know, so I came back . . . I dodged Ma and Pa Smithson easily enough, but they've gone raving mad, stamping about and swearing they'll skin us all alive . . . Where are those kids, by the way, and what was in that note?"

Peter laughed and took him by the arm.

"Come and see, Thomas dear. We've got a surprise for you. Dickie and Mary have found some treasure."

9. *Rain*

WHEN JENNY LEFT Tom she ran down into the clearing, past the Smithsons' camp and into the wood. It was dark under the trees and she had no breath left to shout, so all she could do was to make for the road and hope that she would see Mr Wilkins there. She was near the edge of the wood when a bus passed along the road and she remembered that this would be the first one of the day going to Shrewsbury through Barton Beach. She made a desperate spurt when she heard it stopping, but when she stumbled off the grass verge on to the road she was just in time to see Mr Wilkins boarding it about three hundred yards away. She shouted and waved, but the bus moved on and there seemed nothing to do but stand in the middle of the road without even trying to check the tears of disappointment. What was the best thing to do now?

But luck was really with Jenny for five minutes later a car came up and when she waved frantically it pulled into the side. The driver was a pleasant-looking young woman and she agreed to catch up the bus which Jenny said she had missed. As they drove off the woman looked at her curiously and was about to ask her a question when suddenly the heavens opened and Jenny hastily got on to the subject of weather.

The rain lashed down and but for the windscreen-wiper Jenny would not have known when they passed through Barton. Soon after, they overtook the bus, and she said:

"If you wouldn't mind putting me down at the next bus-stop, that would do beautifully."

She thanked her driver as charmingly as she knew and waved till her car was out of sight. The bus stopped at her signal, and as soon as she got on she realized that Mr

Wilkins was not there. He was easy enough to describe and the conductor remembered that he had got off at Barton.

"I'm so sorry," poor Jenny said, "but you'll have to stop again. I must go back and find him. It's very urgent."

So she jumped off and started to walk back. She had nothing with which to keep out the rain, and already her sweater was sticking to her shoulders. Then she saw another car approaching in a shower of spray and realized that it was Barton's only taxi, driven by an old friend. She waved him to a stop.

"Bless me, if it ain't young Jen Harman," Bill said cheerfully. "Where are you going and what you been doing? You look cold and wet. Better get back home. Sorry I can't take you, but I got a passenger."

Jenny peeped through the window, and suddenly shouted with joy. In the far corner of the car, looking very thin, frail and tired, was Mr Wilkins. She flung open the door and flopped down on the seat beside him.

"Drive on, Bill," she shouted. "Wherever you're going will do for me, because I know Mr Wilkins and we're going to spend the day together . . . Don't you know me, Mr Wilkins? It's Jenny. I've been chasing you all the morning."

A gentle smile lit up the old man's face.

"I know you, child, and I know you for a friend who is not too busy to be kind to an old man. But what are you doing here, miles from home and without a coat? Would you like the driver to take you back?"

Meanwhile, Bill, in spite of Jenny's instructions, had stopped the car and was looking round inquiringly.

"What shall I do, sir?" he asked, but before Mr Wilkins could answer Jenny said:

"*Please* let me come with you, Mr Wilkins. I don't care where you're going if you'll come back with me presently. I came out to find you. I saw you"—and here she put her lips to his ear and whispered so that Bill could not hear—"I saw you get out of that caravan and jump on the bus. Do make him drive on and then I'll tell you everything."

Mr Wilkins looked worried, but her appeal was so earnest that he relented.

"Very well, child. You may come with me if you wish. I am going to Shrewsbury on urgent and important business, but your company will not be unwelcome. Proceed, driver!"

So while Bill proceeded Jenny told Mr Wilkins nearly everything that had happened since he had slipped out of the post office at Barton Beach yesterday morning.

"And do please understand," she finished, "that we are all here to help you. We've got our camp in a cave at the top of the dingle and nobody can stop us. We've all got permission to be away from home and be there. Early this morning Tom and me came down to rescue you, but you were too quick for us, because we saw you breaking open the door of the caravan . . . . Will you tell me, Mr Wilkins, *did they lock you in?*"

The old man looked at her reflectively.

"They did, child . . . They want me to find Roman treasure for them, but I have now made up my mind to have nothing more to do with them. I have finished with them, Jenny . . . Completely finished . . ."

"Really finished?" she asked. "D'you mean you'll leave them altogether?"

"I do, Jenny, and you have helped me to this decision, for not only have I broken a door to escape, but you and your friends, with your courage and loyalty, have made me see what I should do!"

"And will you come back with me presently, when you've done what you've got to do, and stay in our camp and let us help you and protect you?"

"Perhaps I will, child, but first we go to Shrewsbury to find a man called Henry Ringway, who is one of the greatest experts in the world on Roman Britain . . . You shall come with me, child . . . Have you still the spoon?"

She nodded. "Do you know this man, Mr Wilkins?"

"I had a letter from him today. Your mother had kept it for me until I called. I have his address in my pocket."

After that everything that happened was rather confusing, and Jenny was never able to recall the precise order of events. She remembered driving through the streets of Shrewsbury in relentless rain, with Mr Wilkins fidgeting beside her, until they reached an old-fashioned house with a gravel drive leading to the front door. Almost before she realized it she was perched on the edge of a large chair in a book-lined study. Mr Wilkins, talking hard, was next to her, while on the other side of the fire a cheerful little round-faced man with a bald head and steel-rimmed glasses sat smiling at them both. This was Mr Ringway, the great expert on Roman Britain, and he was very pleasant and polite to Jenny and not at all curious about her bedraggled appearance nor why she happened to be with Mr Wilkins. She heard the latter say that he believed the remains of a Roman villa might be found in Greystone Dingle.

"And now, my dear Ringway," Mr Wilkins went on, "I want to show you what my young friend here has in her possession. I feel confident you will confirm my verdict that it is genuine. Jenny and a friend of hers bought it cheaply at an auction sale in Bishop's Castle . . . Now, my dear, will you show your treasure?"

So once again Jenny performed her famous diving trick and pulled up her precious spoon on its ribbon, and if Mr Ringway was a little astonished, he was gentleman enough not to show it. But when he had examined the spoon under a strong desk-lamp and whispered to Mr Wilkins about it, and looked at pictures in a book and scraped the metal and peered at it through a magnifying glass, he got very excited and stuttered a little.

"Remarkable, my child!" he beamed. "A very remarkable find indeed, and although, of course, my own views must be confirmed, I feel confident that this is genuine. You should not carry it like that, my child. It is too valuable. Will you trust me with it?"

But Jenny shook her head and restored her treasure to its hiding-place.

"I'm sorry, sir, but I can't do that. My friend gave it to

me and I've made a sort of vow not to give it up until we've found Mr Wilkins's treasure . . . I do hope you're going to help us to do that? I don't think he's explained that there are six of us all pledged to help him, but we don't know as much about these things as you do."

Mr Ringway put a hand on her shoulder and said, "Yes, of course I'll help, and when Mr Wilkins has told me some more, maybe we'll both agree to let you help too . . . Now you must come and see Mrs Ringway and have a piece of cake and a wash and borrow a coat . . . Come along!"

Jenny never did know what Mr Wilkins told his friend about the Smithsons, but when she returned to the study both men were looking very serious—so serious that she was afraid that they had perhaps decided against the Lone Piners.

"May we start now, please?" she said brightly. "Mrs Ringway has lent me an oilskin like a tent and a sou'wester that slips over my ears, and I shall be quite warm and dry. . . . Will you please both come to our camp in the cave now and make plans with the others? If you want digging we'll dig for you if you tell us where, and then, of course, we're very good at keeping guard . . ." She paused and looked anxiously at Mr Wilkins, and then said quietly, "Have you told him about the Smithsons and the caravan? You will excuse me asking, won't you?"

Mr Wilkins smiled gently. "He knows, Jenny. He is coming with us in a few minutes, but I have told him that others would like me to search for them and that they are not to be trusted. As soon as the rain stops we shall begin to search, but we are going somewhere else before the dingle."

It was still raining hard when they got into Mr Ringway's little car. Jenny sat in front with him, and when she told him that she lived at Barton Beach he nodded and said, "I know. Mr Wilkins told me that your family had befriended him. Do you know the Sterlings of Seven Gates—particularly Charles?"

"Of course I do. We all adore Charles, and his father is

Peter's uncle . . . But you don't know Peter, do you? Her real name is Petronella. She is one of my friends."

"That's splendid," said Mr Ringway. "We're going to Seven Gates first because Charles Sterling knows more about these hills and valleys than anyone I know, and from what I hear of him he'll help too."

When at last they came to Seven Gates, Charles was standing in the doorway of one of the barns, watching the rain. Jenny jumped out first and landed in a deep puddle. It was not surprising that Charles failed to recognize her, as the borrowed mackintosh and hat made a very adequate disguise, but he gave her a suitable welcome when she removed her sou'wester. Then she introduced the men, and Charles said that he knew Mr Ringway well by name and was there anything he could do? They told him promptly that there was and that they wanted to talk to him urgently, so Jenny, very tactfully, dashed off into the kitchen.

Mrs Sterling was baking and her face was hot and flushed as she turned from the oven door at Jenny's "Hello, Aunt Carol! I've got news for you."

"Nobody drowned yet, I hope? What's happened, Jenny? And what on earth are you wearing?"

Jenny laughed as she slipped out of the borrowed oil-skin.

"I can't begin to tell you about the marvellous adventure we've found," she began. "It's going to be so exciting that I can hardly believe it. I've come in a car with two men who are talking to Charles, and he's coming too, and just anything may happen at any moment now . . . The others? Oh, they're all right, Aunt Carol. Of course they are. They're safe and sound and dry in a secret camp in a cave. . . . And I forget if you know about Mr Wilkins, but he's escaped from the caravan and he's one of the men outside . . ."

"Stop! Stop, you crazy child!" Mrs Sterling cried, with her hands over her ears. "Stay here while I go and talk to these men . . . Help yourself to a cake."

So Jenny sat on the kitchen table, happily swinging her legs, and burned her mouth on a piping hot cake. Presently Charles came in and sat on the other end of the table and looked at her seriously.

"Now, young lady! I have an idea that there is a lot behind this story that I don't know about. I like your old Mr Wilkins, and Mr Ringway seems to think he's on to something, but I want to know what you youngsters are up to. Where are you all? And how is it you are by yourself? It's not like you, Jenny . . . I don't know where the two Mr Sterlings have gone off on their own this morning, but my stepmother is trying to persuade me to bring all you children back here to camp in the barn . . . She seems to think you'll all die of pneumonia and that she's responsible to your mums."

"But, *Charles*!" Jenny said tragically, "this is *awful*. You'll never make us come back now, will you? You wouldn't be so horribly, impossibly beastly as that."

"Never mind all that tragic stuff, Jenny. It doesn't work with me. Just tell me where you are and what you're all supposed to be doing."

Jenny looked at him soulfully, but it seemed to make no difference, so she gulped and told him everything.

"Very well, Jen," Charles said at last. "I believe you. I have an idea we ought to hurry, for your pals may be in trouble by now and the rain is worse than ever. I don't remember rain like this for years . . ."

Mr Ringway's little car was soon packed with extra blankets, rope and dry kindling. Then, at the last minute, Mrs Sterling appeared with two big baskets.

"I disapprove of this ridiculous escapade," she said grimly. "But as none of you will listen to me I can't very well allow you all to starve. I've scraped some food together for the party . . ."

They all waved cheerfully as the car moved off across the farmyard which was now a sheet of water. The relentless rain beat down unceasingly. "Surely," Jenny thought, "there has not been rain like this since Noah built his ark."

Five minutes later the rain unaccountably stopped and a watery and apologetic sun appeared as they came into Barton.

"Perhaps it will be better if we don't stop at the post office," Charles said. And Jenny smiled at him gratefully. She had dreaded that they would drop her off.

The clouds were so low that it was nearly dark when they reached the entrance to the dingle, but the rain still held off.

"We'll have to get the car as far up as we can, Ringway," Charles said, "but there'll be a lot of water coming down here soon. I don't like the look of it."

"But Charles," Jenny said, "the Smithsons have left their caravan right in the way. We shan't be able to get by. That's why they did it."

"We can't carry all this gear up to the cave, and I don't intend to try. We'll deal with Mr Smithson, and I think I shall enjoy it."

"I think I can manage that," Mr Wilkins said surprisingly. "Let us proceed."

The caravan was still blocking the way, although the car had been moved. Mr Ringway sounded his horn and they all got out. After a few moments the door of the caravan opened and Mrs Smithson appeared. She was looking haggard and miserable, but her expression hardened when she saw Mr Wilkins.

"So you've come back, have you—?" she began, and then stopped as the old man held up his hand and said, "Where is your husband?" in such a firm tone that she answered meekly, "He's somewhere up the valley. He told me to stay here"—her voice rose suddenly on a note of hysteria—"but I don't want to stay here, Uncle. I'm scared here all alone. I hate the rain, and Percy won't come back and I want to go to the police, but he won't let me . . . Will you help me, Uncle?"

The three men looked at each other and then Charles said, "What d'you mean, 'won't come back'?"

"He's been kidnapped," she screamed, "that's what's happened. He's been kidnapped by some gipsy brats and hidden in a cave. I know he has, and nobody will do anything about it. Help me, please."

An embarrassed silence followed this outburst, until Jenny laughed. She could not help it, for she was suddenly sure about the identity of the "gipsy brats."

"Is your husband looking for the boy?" Mr Wilkins asked, and Jenny noticed that for the second time in a few minutes he refused to use their names.

"He's digging," Mrs Smithson laughed bitterly. "Scratching about in the stones up there. The rain stopped him before, but he's more interested in digging than in his own son. I think he's gone crazy."

"Very well," Charles said, "we will go and find him. Stand aside, Mrs Smithson, please, while we move this caravan a few feet so that we can get the car by."

The men pushed the caravan aside while the woman watched them. Suddenly Jenny was sorry for her. She was a pathetic, broken figure.

Charles leaned from the window as Mr Ringway started his car again.

"Those children camping at the top are friends of mine, and maybe your boy is with them. If he is, I give you my word he'll be with you in half an hour. And I shall advise your husband to come back at once and move your car and caravan without delay. They're not safe where they are."

"Not safe?" the woman echoed. "Why?"

"There may be a lot of water coming down this valley soon. You'd better get packed up ready to move at once . . . I'll tell him."

Mr Ringway had great trouble with the car, for although this part of the dingle was wide, the rain had made the ground so slippery that the wheels failed to grip and spun round in the mud. Charles was now very worried and anxious to get to the camp as soon as possible, and several times the three of them got out of the car and pushed. The third time Mr Wilkins said, "I think, if you don't mind, it would be as well to stop the engine here. I have an idea that my nephew may be round the next corner and I should like, if I can, to see what he is doing without him being aware of my presence. Perhaps Jenny would come with me and reconnoitre."

So with thumping heart Jenny took the old man's hand and crept forward until they reached the shelter of a large rock which jutted across half the track. Slowly Jenny moved her head until she could see round the bend. Then, with a gasp of surprise, she turned her head and whispered, "You were right. Look!"

What they saw was a sorry sight. This part of the dingle was fairly wide and flat, with many more stones than grass. Standing near to them, in the middle of the stones, was Mr Smithson. Beside him lay a pickaxe and a large hoe, but he was using—very violently and ineffectively—a heavy spade. He seemed to be trying to *dig*, but loose stones are not easy to dig. They almost resent it, and although he seemed to want to get down several feet, he had made little progress so far. His face was scarlet and gleaming with perspiration.

Then it began to rain hard again and Mr Wilkins drew Jenny back to the others.

"I was correct in my surmise. He is there and is digging haphazardly like a lunatic, just where I hoped he would not. He must be removed from that spot at once, Ringway. That is imperative."

"Shall I charge him if I can get round the corner?" the cheerful Mr Ringway grinned. "Let's go . . ."

He started the engine as Charles went on ahead.

"Good afternoon," he said quietly, and had the pleasure of seeing Smithson drop his spade in surprise.

"Who are you?" the latter began, and then stopped when the car drove round the corner and Jenny, Wilkins and Ringway got out.

Mr Wilkins spoke first.

"There is nothing to argue about and nothing to discuss.

125

I have finished with you. My friend, Mr Sterling, has something important to tell you, and I suggest that for once you try to listen without arguing."

Charles was still unsmiling as he spoke: "I'm warning you to move your car and caravan right away from your present camp. Get them out on the road and away. It'll be safer for you if you do. I warned Mrs Smithson on the way up."

"What d'you mean? Why should I move? Who are you, anyway, to give orders?"

"I tell you it's not safe there, but you can please yourself if you wish . . . There'll be a lot of water coming down this dingle soon, and your caravan is on the lowest part. You're asking for trouble."

"There's no stream down there," Smithson sulked. "It disappears higher up—round the next bend . . . This is a trick. You just want me out of the way . . . I'm staying here."

Charles shrugged.

"Very well. I've warned you. We're going farther up. If your son is with my young friends I'll send him back to you. Right, Mr Ringway. We'll try again."

They left Smithson staring after them suspiciously, but it was evident, even to Jenny, that he was impressed by his uncle's change of manner and also by the two men with him. As they disappeared round the next bend he looked as if he knew that he had been fooled.

But round the next corner was as far as Mr Ringway could get the car.

"That's it," Charles said as he got out. "Now we must unload and carry everything. Run on ahead, Jenny, and tell the others that the rescue-party has arrived and that they had better come and rescue us."

So Jenny hurried on among the rocks and in a minute the car was out of sight. Suddenly she was afraid. The dark sky seemed to be pressing down on her between the hills, and as she clenched her teeth to stop them chattering, the rain swept down the valley like a fog and blotted out everything but the rocks a few yards ahead. Surely it could not be far to the cave now? Surely the others would hear her if she whistled the peewit call?

Suddenly she stopped and screamed in terror as a shape came blundering through the mist towards her. Then she recognized Peter—white-faced, breathless and as near panic and hysteria as she would ever be.

In relief Jenny laughed and called her name, but Peter staggered forward and fell against her, sobbing.

"Jenny!" she gasped. "Oh, Jenny! It's awful, Jen! . . . Quickly! . . . We must get help quickly."

"But what is it, Peter? What's wrong?"

"We must find Charles and lots of men to help us, Jenny. *But we must hurry.* Help me, Jenny! . . ."

"But why? What's wrong, Peter?"

"The twins and that Percy! They've fallen down a hole in the mine inside the mountain and the pit is filling with water . . ."

10. The Cave

"WHERE'S JENNY?" David called down to Tom as, with Peter, he toiled up the steep track to the cave. "Everything all right?"

"I hope so," Tom puffed. And he repeated the story he had told Peter.

"Come on, Tom," said Peter, tugging at his sleeve. "Look at the surprise we've been keeping for you . . . Just see what we've got," and she turned and ran into the cave, calling for Mary and Dickie.

From the gloomy interior came a strange procession. First, Dickie, holding in his right hand the end of a rope, to the other end of which was attached Powerless Percy— gagged and bound by the wrists. Behind the prisoner Mackie trotted and then Mary, looking very smug, who put out her tongue at Tom when she noticed his look of disapproval.

But it was Peter who stepped forward and pulled the sock from Percy's mouth and said sharply to Dickie:

"I don't think that was funny, twins. There was no need for a gag, and, if David agrees, I suggest you untie his wrists. He can't run away."

Dickie sulked. "That's all very well, but he's our prisoner and doesn't belong to anyone else. We're going to swop him for Mr Wilkins . . . Anyway, that gag wasn't tied too tight and the rope didn't hurt, did it, Percy?"

To everyone's astonishment the prisoner smiled feebly and shook his head. "Didn't hurt me. I don't care what tricks you silly kids play. I'm not scared. What are you going to do to me, anyway?"

"I'll tell you what we're *not* going to do, young Percy. We're not going to tie up darling Mackie and let you throw rocks at him . . . You made a big mistake when you threw stones at Mackie. I gave you good warning that you'd be sorry."

"All right, Mary," David said. "Never mind about that now. Take off that rope and we'll see what he knows."

A flicker of apprehension showed in Percy's pale eyes at the last sentence, but he held his wrists forward.

"Do you know what a parole means?" David asked as he loosened the knots.

Percy looked at him suspiciously. "No, I don't, and I don't reckon as I wants to know either. What's the catch? . . . And you'd better all be careful, else I'll tell my father that you've been bullying me."

Dickie thrust his small, pugnacious face forward until it was within a few inches of Percy's.

"Ha! ha!" he intoned with a frightful sneer. "So you're going to tell your daddy that two weak little twins—one of 'em a girl—captured you and tied you up all by themselves and bullied you? Just you try that on, Sir Percy the Brave, and we'll follow you to the end of the world. Won't we, twin?"

Mary placed her head close to Dickie's and glared at Percy so that he shrank back.

"A very amusing performance," David said as he pulled the twins back with a hand on each of their collars. "Now, young Percy, just listen while I tell you about a parole . . . A parole is a prisoner's promise that he will not attempt to escape under certain conditions. We don't want to keep you tied up here particularly, but we've made up our minds that you're going to stay our prisoner until we know that Mr Wilkins is safe and sound. If you give your parole that you won't try to escape, I'll take those ropes off you and you can help us about the camp. If you don't promise we'll have to tie you up again. What's it to be?"

Percy looked round nervously. The twins were still glaring hatred at him. Tom regarded him as if he were some strange animal, and David with genuine curiosity. Peter was busy cooking at the camp-fire, but when she looked up at David's question the boy thought he saw a gleam of pity in her eyes. It was just like the warm-hearted Peter to be sorry for him now that they had him a prisoner.

"Suppose I don't promise," he muttered.

"There's no end to this cave," Dickie said. "It just goes on an' on, an' down an' down into the mountain, gettin' darker an' darker . . ."

"If you don't promise we'll tie you up a long way back in the cave," Mary added. "Almost as far as the bowels of the mountain right underneath the Devil's Chair."

Percy was worried. Never in his wildest dreams had he imagined that anything like this could happen to him.

"All right," he said sulkily, "I'll do whatever you call it. Untie my hands properly."

"You promise not to escape?" David persisted. "Promise not to leave this camping place?"

"Do you swear?" Tom said.

"All you have to do is to give your word of honour," Peter said. "I wish you would really promise, because it will make it much easier for us all."

"I've told you," Percy replied peevishly. "How many times have I got to say it. I promise."

"You're crackers, David," Dickie said as he turned his back. "That Percy doesn't know what honour means. You've spoiled everything. He'll trick us."

"Of course he will," Mary sniffed. "All we can do is to stand so close to him wherever he goes that he daren't break his word. We promised to swop him for Mr Wilkins, and we're going to keep him safe to swop, however silly you others are. We don't trust him."

David undid the rope and threw it on the floor of the cave while Percy rubbed his wrists.

"Now," said David, "you can help us to get in some wood before it rains again. Everything is so wet that it will be difficult to keep a fire going soon."

"I thought you said I wasn't to go away from the camp. You don't know what you do mean."

"Don't worry, Percy dear," Mary said. "We shall go

with you—and Mackie too. We'll take an axe and go and find some dead wood, and we'll chop and you can carry."

"And even if you have given your parole," Dickie said, "you might just as well try and be a bit polite. Don't speak so rudely to our big brother."

Tom grinned and passed Dickie the axe.

"Before you go there's something I want to ask Percy," he said. "Why did your people lock Mr Wilkins in the caravan? You couldn't keep him a prisoner all the time, anyway, and what had he done?"

Percy did not like Tom. Nor did he like his straight way of talking and the unfriendly look in his eye.

"He hadn't done anything to us," he muttered, and then turned to the twins. "Aren't we going for wood?"

"Just a sec," David said. "If Mr Wilkins hadn't done anything to you all, why did you keep him against his will, and why was he locked in the caravan?"

"Pop often told me that the old man didn't know what he was doing or saying."

"Do you think that?" Peter said as she stood up from the fire. "We think he's a dear old man."

Percy had no answer to this, and when David nodded, Dickie picked up the axe, smiled brightly at the prisoner on parole, and led the way down into the dingle with Mackie and Mary following.

Three times within the next hour Percy and one of the twins returned to the cave with fuel, and on each occasion it seemed to the others that he became more human. Soon after it began to rain hard again, and when they ran for the shelter of the cave Percy slipped on the muddy track leading up to the plateau. Dickie hauled him to his feet, and when he saw his mud-streaked face began to roar with laughter.

"Pity your mother can't see you now," Peter heard him say, and was then astonished when Percy laughed too and said:

"She don't really care for me going out in the rain."

Then, when he reached the cave and saw Peter smiling at him, he came forward, looked into the cooking-pot and said, "I'm hungry. When do we eat?"

"When the cook says so and not before," Tom replied, and then caught Dickie's eye, winked and jerked his head towards the back of the cave.

Dickie looked suspicious. "Why are you pulling faces, Tom? Have you got a pain?"

"Nothing to the pain you'll be having if you don't do as you're told," Tom replied. "Take him to the back of the cave for a bit—quickly!"

"No, you don't," Percy said. "I've given my promise not to escape and that ought to be good enough."

"What's the idea, Tom?" David asked as his friend peered cautiously round the edge of the cave and looked down the dingle.

"It doesn't matter now," he said. "I thought I saw Mr Smithson peep round that rock down there just now and then dodge back . . . I was right. Here they come . . . Keep Percy in the background until we know what they've got to say."

"Sorry, Tom," David said. "I didn't see them . . . We can't really stop them taking Percy—"

"If they really want him," Tom murmured.

"—but if we all stick together and answer them back and keep in front of Percy they might get in a fearful rage and even go away . . . We can't do much really, but I don't want either of them to pass the entrance to the cave *whatever they say or do*. This camp is ours, and we must stay here until Jenny comes back."

During this speech Mary watched Percy carefully and was surprised to notice that the news of his parents' approach did not seem to thrill him. Strangely enough, he neither called out nor tried to escape as the Lone Piners stood before their camp-fire in a silent semi-circle, waiting for the two grown-ups as they struggled up the dingle towards them.

Mr Smithson spoke first. "Now, kids," he began, "just

132

listen to me and be reasonable. This isn't a game. It's a real serious matter, and we want to make things easy for you . . . You've had your bit of fun, and as I like my bit o' fun we'll say no more about it. First of all, tell me where that crazy old uncle of mine has gone, because we've got to find him quick, and then you can finish your kids' games and young Percy can come back with us . . . I know he's here because I saw him just now."

Silence greeted this speech. David knew that there was not much to say, anyway, and the others made no comment, remembering that they were to make the enemy angry if they could.

"You've got him hidden," Mrs Smithson screeched suddenly. "We know you 'ave. Bring him out and we won't do anything about sending for the police——"

This was David's chance.

"Are you really going to send for a policeman?" he asked quietly. "If he comes perhaps you'll ask him to come up here. We've been wondering when we ought to tell the police what we know about Mr Wilkins."

"An' what do you know?" Smithson blurted.

Tom took up the tale.

"When we ran down to your camp before breakfast we saw Mr Wilkins forcing his way out of your caravan. We thought perhaps we ought to let the police know that *he'd been locked in.*"

"Maybe that's why you want the police?" David remarked. "If you want to talk to them about that there's no need for us to do so, but I expect they'll like to know what Tom saw . . . Was there anything else you wanted?"

"Listen," Smithson gasped. "Listen, kids. I'm trying to be patient and I'm trying to play fair. The fun is all over now. *Do any of you know where Mr Wilkins has gone?* It's urgent. I gotta know in a hurry." He brought out a bulging wallet. "I'd pay good money to know where that old man has gone."

David flushed with anger, but Peter smiled sweetly. "But surely you said he was in your charge and that you're looking after him? Surely he wouldn't want to run away if you're so kind to him?"

"Never mind about answering that brat's smart questions," Mrs Smithson shouted. "It's Percy I want . . . Aren't you man enough to deal with kids? Go up there and fetch Percy. Make them give him up."

Her husband regarded her distastefully.

"Listen, kids," he began again. "Tell me where Wilkins is and I'll say nothing more and pay you for your trouble."

"But *Percy*," Mrs Smithson wailed. "It's Percy we want. Go up there and get him."

At this stage, just when David was wondering what to do next, Percy saved him by pushing between Peter and Tom and speaking to his parents.

"Say or do what you like, Pop," he began with his usual courtesy, "but I'm not coming down there with you now."

"*Not coming*, my precious?" his mother cried. "*Of course* you're coming. You can't stay here with these horrible children who have been ill-treating you . . . They *have* been ill-treating you, haven't they?"

Here Dickie threw back his head and released what he hoped was a laugh of scorn.

"We'll swop him for Mr Wilkins like we said in the note. No Mr Wilkins, no Percy," he said tersely.

"Be quiet, Dickie," David snapped as Mrs Smithson cried:

"Did you hear that? They admit it! It's kidnapping, that's what it is." Then she lifted her voice again: "Come home with us now, my precious boy. Your father will see that they don't hurt you again."

But Percy could smell stew bubbling in the pot behind him and he was very hungry. He also felt that the Lone Piners were despising him for the way his mother was behaving, and he had an idea that he wanted to show them that he was not so feeble as they thought. They had indeed already done something for him!

"It's no good, Ma," he said. "I'm not coming with you yet. I like these kids. I like it here."

"You don't!" Mary gasped indignantly. "You hate us. You've jolly well got to hate us. We hate you. How dare you say you like us?"

"But I do. I like you specially, Mary. You're the nicest girl I ever met. I want to stay up here with you . . . You promised I could share your camp."

Dickie was horrified at the expression on his sister's face.

"But you *can't* do that," he said. "You just can't like us. . . . Why, we *tortured* you."

"Tortured!" Mrs Smithson wailed.

"Yes, they did," Percy boasted. "They tied me to a tree and fixed a tin with a hole in the bottom over my head and filled the tin with water."

"It's an Indian torture," Mary explained brightly. "The idea is that a drop of water keeps on droppin' out slowly on the victim's head an' he goes mad waitin' for the next drop."

"But this didn't work very well this time," Dickie said. "The hole was too big and the water ran out quickly. The thing to do is to stuff the hole with a match-end . . . We'll get it right next time, Percy."

And Percy actually grinned.

"You come here at once, Perce," his father said, "and no more o' that silly nonsense."

"I'm not coming. I've given my promise."

"Don't worry about that," David said hurriedly. "We release you from your parole. Maybe you'd better go with your parents."

Suddenly Percy was an embarrassment to the Lone Piners. Once they wanted him, but now, because he wished to stay, it was better that he should go. It seemed as if Percy had been very cunning. Or was it only greed because Peter's stew smelled so good?

Mr Smithson looked as if he was going to explode.

"For the last time, Perce," he bellowed, "come down 'ere and stop playing the fool."

"I'm not coming. I've never had any friends like this before. I'm staying in this camp."

Then his father made the mistake of trying to rush up the muddy track to fetch his erring son. The path was steep and slippery, and because Mr Smithson's shoes were not intended for walks in the wet countryside he slipped and fell heavily on his face. When at last he raised his great bulk from the ground his face was streaked and his clothes plastered with mud.

Macbeth barked wildly. Mr Smithson then lost control of himself. He began to stamp and swear and then he picked up a large stone and flung it at the little dog. Luckily he missed.

"Seek him, Mackie," Mary whispered. "Seek him out," and with a wild yelp of triumph Macbeth charged into battle. But the fight was short, for the dog had every advantage at close quarters.

After a couple of minutes Percy watched his parents' retreat with an unpleasant sneer on his face.

"Serve 'em right," he said, and not one of the others ever forgave him for that.

"I'm glad we can't hear what they're saying," Peter murmured, and then they were all saved the embarrassment of speaking to Percy by the arrival of a cocky Macbeth. They made much of him and then looked at each other blankly as they realized that Percy now expected to be treated as an ally.

"There's no need for you all to keep staring at me," he said as they fidgeted about while Peter prodded the potatoes in the stew. "I meant what I said. I'd much rather stay here with you. I'll do anything you want and take my share of the jobs."

"We'll see to that," Dickie said. "Don't you worry about that, Percy pet."

Mary's wide eyes followed him around and stared him out when he tried to meet them.

"I knew we were wrong to untie you and let you have that parole," she said quietly. "I don't trust you, Percy . . . And don't you ever dare say again that you like me."

"But I do," he said, and then was a little abashed when she turned her back on him and walked away.

The meal round the camp-fire was not a success, although Peter's stew was excellent. Percy had several helpings and did not mind asking for what he wanted. The others were quiet, largely because they did not feel they could discuss their affairs while he was with them. The three older ones were all anxious about Jenny, and Peter, in particular, was getting depressed about the weather.

Suddenly the rain swept down the dingle with renewed fury. In a few seconds the rocky hillside opposite was blotted out and, as the wind veered a trifle, the lashing, silver spears of rain reached their camp-fire at the cave's entrance and hissed among the embers.

"This won't do," David said. "We must move right inside. Everybody take what they can." And they all moved their gear farther back into shelter.

"We ought to keep a fire going," Peter said. "Let's light another farther inside the cave and risk the smoke being a nuisance. We must move all the bedding farther back too, and if it goes on raining like this you boys will have to sleep inside. I'm worried that we may not have enough dry wood, David. We can't stay here without a fire, and we can't move out in this rain. I don't ever remember rain like this."

"I'm worried about Jenny," David replied, "and I'm worried about the whole adventure. We're just not *doing* anything, and we can't do anything until she comes back with or without Mr Wilkins."

Dickie then had a bright idea and suggested that they take torches and really explore the passage at the back of the cave.

"Yes, let's do that," David agreed. "It's no use just sitting about here."

"And what about Jen?" Tom said indignantly. "Suppose she comes back while we're all fiddling about up there. She'll think we've broken our promise."

They all laughed at him for this, but he would not agree

to join the explorers until they had written Jenny a note and put it on a stone near the fire.

"We shan't be long, anyway," David said, "but we might just as well have a look round. I'll just add a line to tell her to put the kettle on."

They each had a torch—Percy was allowed to take Jenny's—and as the twins already knew some of the passage Dickie went first with David, and Peter at his heels. Tom went next with Percy, and Mary, with a rather unhappy Macbeth, last.

The floor was treacherous with fallen stones, and the rocky walls and roof dripped moisture, but after going forward very cautiously for about fifteen yards the passage began to run uphill. Suddenly Dickie stopped.

"Something's happened here," he said. "The main passage is all blocked up with rocks. This must be where the roof fell in."

David swung his torch up and across to the left, and then, with a note of excitement in his voice, said:

"There's a stiff draught coming from somewhere . . . Look down, Dickie. Surely there's an opening of some sort on the left here and in the floor too? . . . Use your own torch, but be careful."

David was correct. At one time the gallery here must have forked right and left, and the falling roof had completely blocked one passage and half covered the other which ran steeply downhill.

Dickie was squealing with excitement as he squeezed past a piece of broken rock and disappeared into the unknown. The others followed quickly.

There were not so many stones underfoot here and the air smelled colder and fresher and almost at once they became aware of a strange, muffled roar somewhere below them. They were all very excited as Tom said:

"Wish I knew what that noise was."

Even while he was asking the question David supplied the answer. "It's running water. A waterfall or something. Shall we go on?"

Peter squeezed his arm.

"Of course. But watch how you go. We don't want to fall into something. Keep an eye on those kids."

The roar of falling water was now unmistakable and David was not surprised when the gallery turned sharply to the left and they found themselves standing on a rocky platform some fifteen or twenty feet above a pool, the water in which seethed and foamed under the impact of a waterfall which crashed into it at one end.

David turned and yelled to the little group behind him: "All torches on at the same time so that we can really see what's happening."

Six beams of light swept upwards and just picked out the lip of the waterfall high above them in the roof of the great cave. Then David led the way along the gallery to the opposite end and stopped by a wall of rock about four feet above the present level of the water.

"There's a space between the wall of the cave and that ridge of rock," Tom pointed. "I reckon that the pool would overflow over that when it's full and run away somewhere else."

Then the beams swung down and across the lake to show them that the platform on which they were standing was directly above a little "beach" of rough stones about three feet wide. Apart from this beach, the pool covered the whole area of this mysterious cave.

"Save the batteries," David said. "I'll just keep my torch on for a bit. This is the rummiest place I've ever been in."

"Have you noticed that the water is not really *clear*?" Peter shouted. "It's muddy, and I don't believe it's been running in here very long, else it would be overflowing the other end."

Before David could answer, Percy raised his voice in complaint.

"I'm cold and I don't feel very well. I'd like to go back now, if you don't mind."

"*We* don't mind," Dickie yelled with a fiendish grin.

"It's just what we'd like . . . You go, Percy dear, and we'll stay and explore this place."

He did not go, of course, and Mary said, "P'raps you bigger ones would kindly move a bit so that we can look over the edge. We really found this place. It was our idea, as *usual*, to go and explore these old mines, and now you go bossing around and giving orders and gettin' in the way; just because we're smaller we're kept out of everything . . . Excuse me, *please*!"

Nobody was ever quite sure what happened next, but Dickie did admit later that as he pushed forward with Mary he made a playful grab at Percy's arm. Percy then lost his head and began to struggle.

"Look out, you little idiots!" Tom yelled as Percy fell against Mary, who was caught off her balance and toppled over the edge. Dickie snatched at her just too late, slipped on the wet rock, grabbed at Percy to save himself, and the two of them followed Mary and crashed on to the shingle beach below.

The cave was filled with the roaring of waters which smothered Percy's despairing cry and Peter's sob of fear. For ten terrible seconds the two older boys stared dumbly at each other. David recovered first, although he was not conscious of the fierce grip of Peter's hands round his arm.

"Shine your torches down," he yelled, "and take care not to slip yourselves."

Three rather shaky beams of yellow light wavered down to the little beach. Percy was sitting with his hands round one ankle. Dickie and Mary were both scrambling to their feet—the former with blood and a bruise on his forehead, and the latter rubbing her elbow. They both smiled shakily at the others and Mary shouted, "Take care of Mackie, David. He's trying to jump down."

Peter felt a lump rise in her throat in recognition of Mary's courage and unselfishness.

Tom grabbed Mackie and lifted the dog's trembling little body in his arms.

"All right, old chap," he murmured into his rough coat. "Don't fuss. We'll get them up."

But how? The walls of the cave had been smoothed by the action of water through the centuries. They could not reach down and pull them up, and even if one of them jumped down and tried to lift the youngsters up in turn there was risk that the rescuer himself would never be able to get back. David remembered that Dickie's piece of rope which had been left in the cave above would be no help, as it was far too thin and short.

"Sure you're all right?" Peter called. "What about you, Dickie? You've got a big bump coming up on your forehead."

"I'm all right, thanks, Peter. How are you going to get us out—I'm hungry."

Try as he would, David could not conquer a sick feeling of fear as he smiled down at his brother. "We'll get you out, Richard. Don't worry."

"We're not worrying yet," Mary added, "but I think you ought to do something soon, 'cos I'm quite sure the water in this pool is rising quickly."

And it was true that during the last few minutes the sound of the waterfall had deepened as more and more flood-water poured into the pool. David was sure that they had found the source of some great underground river, and that unless they could get the twins and Percy out fairly soon the water would rise over their heads *before* it reached the natural overflow.

Dickie looked up at David. "What we want is a good ladder and some rope and then we'll soon be on our way. But you might hurry. It's getting cold down here and there's too much water."

"It's rising fast," Mary called. "Really fast. It's over all the stones now and over my shoes. Please do something. I don't like it."

David looked despairingly at Peter, who seemed suddenly to pull herself together as she said, "Stay here with Tom and try and think of something. I'll find my way up with my torch and get help somehow. Help them to be brave, David!"

11. *The Secret River*

JENNY HAD NEVER seen Peter lose control of herself before, and as the elder girl clung to her gasping for breath she forgot her own distress and fear.

"But Peter, what do you mean—the pit is filling with water and the twins are in it?"

Peter took her arm from Jenny's shoulder and rubbed a grubby hand across her wet forehead. She was still too breathless to speak properly.

"Sorry, Jenny!" she gasped at last. "We must get some strong rope because we've found a hidden lake under the mountain and the twins and Percy have fallen in and the water is rising fast."

Before she had finished speaking Jenny had turned and was running back the way she had come. Over her shoulder she yelled, "Don't worry, Peter! Charles is here, and I know we've got rope."

Peter could hardly believe her own ears. Suddenly her knees wobbled and she felt horribly sick. What was that Jenny had said about Charles and rope? She must be crazy.

Then she heard the deep voice which she had always loved saying quite calmly, "Buck up, Pete. Just show me the way and we'll fix everything. It'll be all right, my dear, don't worry! You've done all you can and we'll soon have these kids out of trouble."

Peter brushed her hand across her eyes and gave him a shaky but grateful smile.

"You're like a fairy-story come true, Charles." And after this she was the old, cool, resourceful Peter again. She led them through the cave to the passage while Charles told her that Mr Wilkins was safe with them and that they had a new friend in Mr Ringway who had come to help them.

"When Jenny came back for me," he said, "I told the others to unload the car and bring all the stuff into the cave . . . So this is where the roof fell in? Steady with the torch, Peter. I'm a bit big for this hole . . . What's that noise?"

"That's the waterfall," she shouted. "It's filling the lake. . . . *Do hurry*, Charles!"

Then they turned the corner and were on the ledge and Peter shouted above the din, "Don't worry, David. Charles is here with a rope. Are they still all right? . . ." Then suddenly, with a new note of fear in her voice, "Where's David, Tom? I can't see him."

Charles pulled a heavy torch from his pocket just as Tom shone his own on the newcomers. Tom's face was white and glistening, but when he recognized Charles he managed a smile of welcome.

"Nice work, Peter," he yelled. "David's all right. Look! He's flat on his tum encouraging the kids. He doesn't know you're here yet . . . Let down that rope quickly, Charles. The water is over their waists."

"Hold my torch," Charles snapped at Jenny. "Shine it down on the water and keep it steady," and he began to uncoil his rope and fasten one end of it round his own waist.

Peter flopped on her knees beside David and put her hands on his shoulders. He was leaning over the edge of the rocky ledge, without a thought of his own danger, and doing his best to encourage the children below. When David turned his head, saw Peter and heard that Charles was here with a rope, he gave her a smile which she never forgot and a "Thanks, Pete."

"Hold on, kids," David yelled. "We'll have you up in a sec. Charles is here."

"Do hurry, Charles darling," came Mary's plaintive cry. "The water is trying to drag us into it. It's pulling all the time."

"I'll take the strain, David," Charles shouted. "Will you go down on the end of the rope and fix it to each of 'em in turn? Better hurry."

143

In a few seconds David was lowered into the water, which was now over two feet deep, until his feet touched the beach. He knotted the rope round his sister and yelled, "Haul away!"

Up went Mary to safety and down came the rope again for Dickie, who tried to argue that Percy ought to go next as he was the visitor! But he had to go because he was next youngest, and then came the turn of the snivelling Percy.

It was while he was giving Percy a push from below that David felt the swirling water pulling at him more fiercely. For some time now he had realized that the river emptying itself into the pool almost certainly found its way out again through an underground channel below the level of the rock ledge. It was obvious, too, that much more water was coming in than was flowing out.

Down came the rope again and Charles shouted, "Buck up, David. Don't be afraid to hold on to the rope. Tom and Peter and I are all hanging on."

Then up he came, easily enough, and was just trying to wring some of the water out of his trousers when Jenny swung round the beam of Charles's torch and shouted, "What's happening to the water? Over there! By that ledge."

As they watched, the water heaved and boiled as if some subterranean monster was stirring in his sleep.

"It's going to overflow across that ledge," Peter cried. "I'm sure it is . . . And some of the rock is breaking up under the strain . . . It's like a dam breaking."

"Back to the cave," Charles shouted urgently. "Twins first—carry that dog, Mary. I think we've found the underground river of Greystone, which is going to rise and flood the valley and plenty more besides. Those people camping at the bottom had better move quickly, and we must warn Wilkins and Ringway."

As soon as they had squeezed through the narrow opening into the main gallery, and left the horrible sound of rushing water behind them, David and Peter raced ahead into the cave where Mr Wilkins turned and looked at them in astonishment.

"We've got them, Mr Wilkins," Peter shouted. "It's all right now. They're safe, but Charles says we must warn the Smithsons at the bottom of the dingle."

The old man looked bewildered, and when David snapped, "Where's the chap you've brought with you and your car?" he came forward and pointed down the valley. The rain, ironically enough, had stopped now, and it was a little lighter as the rest of the party rushed out of the cave behind them. Charles pushed through the crowd of children, nodded and smiled to Mr Wilkins, and then looked anxiously up the valley. Tom, just behind him, shouted and pointed over his shoulder.

Some forty yards up the dingle, *the very ground was moving*! As they watched they saw some stones shift, a tuft of heather slide over sideways, and then, with a muffled roar, a flood of brown water broke out of the ground.

"That's it!" Charles shouted. "I never believed it, but there it is! The secret river of Greystone!" and then, as he turned and called something to Mr Wilkins, Peter remembered his previous warning, and dashed down the little track from the plateau just as the first uprush of water gathered itself up like an animal preparing to spring. Before the others realized what was happening, she was in the dingle, running with all her strength to warn Mr Ringway and the Smithsons of the peril at her heels. David raced after her but she had a good start, and when he reached the level the flood caught him. He felt the water cold over his shoes, and then saw it surge past him. A heavy stone crashed against his ankle and he stumbled and fell, face forward, in the water. He spat out some mud as he struggled to his feet again and was just in time to see Peter caught in the same way. Dimly he heard Charles roar out a fresh warning from somewhere behind him, and then a new rush of water swept him off his feet. He struck out wildly and, to his astonishment and fear, found himself out of his depth. David could swim well enough—though not so well as

Peter—and after the first shock found himself being carried forward on the crest of the flood. In a few seconds he was swept round a rock and, where the valley widened, saw Peter struggling ashore about twenty yards ahead. At his shout she turned, recognized him, and plunged back into the water. Spluttering and laughing excitedly, she grabbed his arm, and then they both staggered out on to higher ground.

"What did you do that for, you chump?" Peter gasped. "Did you dive off the top?"

"I came after you, you idiot. What did you think you could do by dashing off like that by yourself?"

Once again Peter pointed ahead and David saw a small man standing on a rock which disappeared for a moment in a cloud of spray as it was struck by the torrent.

"That must be Mr Ringway," Peter said, "and there goes his car! Come on, David. We must try and warn the Smithsons." But as they ran they realized that they had little chance of beating the water, and when they came to the clearing, exhausted and breathless, they saw that the water had spread out somewhat, but had been strong enough to swing the caravan sideways and swamp a tent and knock it flat. The car, with Mr and Mrs Smithson, their feet under water, standing disconsolately beside it, looked unharmed. Although the flood was comparatively shallow here, the new river was flowing down fast and steadily and, owing to the lie of the land, split into two streams just by the car. The first was already making a new bed for itself as it tore across the soft ground and pine needles on its way through the wood to the road. The other, not running nearly so fast, took a course parallel to the edge of the wood, and would doubtless make its way to the road eventually.

It was nearly dusk now as they approached the Smithsons and David said, "Good evening. I'm afraid you've had some trouble. Didn't Mr Sterling warn you when he came by this way? . . . Peter here nearly drowned herself trying to race the river to warn you, but the water beat us."

Mrs Smithson regarded them sullenly, while her husband had the grace to look a little abashed.

"Thanks," he said shortly. "Can't understand how all this water come down here, anyway, but there's not much damage done. Either of you two seen my kid Percy? Is he O.K.?"

"He's all right," Peter said, "but you'll find him rather wet. He's been paddling. I think it would be a good idea to get something hot ready for him and a change of clothes too. We'll send him down to you when we get back."

"But you're not going back, Peter," David said. "Someone ought to get back to Seven Gates right away and warn Mrs Sterling that we're in rather a mess. Both you and the twins must get into hot baths—"

"What about you? You're *filthy*, David. Absolutely disgusting."

He laughed and turned to Mr Smithson.

"Look, sir. We're all in trouble now and my friend here is wet through and cold. Will you take her in your car to a farm the other side of Barton and then see if you can get a taxi in the village to come out here right away? We're all wet and shall have to break camp, anyway, and we might as well help each other now instead of fighting."

Peter and Mrs Smithson both started talking together, but Mr Smithson let out a roar of laughter.

"You've got a nerve, my boy. That's the coolest thing I've heard for a long time, but I'll do it. Get in the car, girl, and show me the way . . . And you get something moving in the caravan for young Perce, my dear," he added to his bewildered wife.

"But David," Peter protested, "I can't go now. It's ridiculous. I'm all right. The twins want looking after, not me . . . Anyway, you can't order me about like this!"

"Can't I?" David grinned as he shut the car door. "I'm captain here, and you'll kindly obey orders. Get yourself dry and get H.Q.2 ready for us. Cheerio!"

And as the car squelched off through the mud and water between the trees, Peter sat back with glowing cheeks wondering whether, after all, it was not rather nice to be ordered about by one particular person.

David watched the car until it was out of sight and then realized that Mrs Smithson was still standing feebly in the muddy water swirling past the caravan.

"Anything I can do?" he asked. "Can't you open the door?"

She looked at him dully.

"My Percy is coming soon? Honest? He's not hurt?"

"He's wet and cold because he fell in a small lake. We'll bring him along soon, so don't worry, but you must get something hot ready for him."

She nodded and paused on the steps of the caravan. "And Uncle George? Mr Wilkins?"

"I forgot about him. He's fine, but he's staying with us," and with that parting shot he turned and went back up the dingle. It seemed a long way to the cave, for he was tired and cold and wet. The rain started again too, just as if there wasn't enough water about already, and it was nearly dark when he passed Mr Ringway's deserted car and whistled the peewit call. As soon as he had rounded the corner he had to wade again through the rushing water, but he was certain that the current was not now so strong. He looked up towards the cave, saw the gleam of flames and heard the hum of voices.

Jenny was the first to see him as he climbed wearily up the track to the little plateau, but the others crowded round him with questions as he went up to the welcome fire. He told them what he had done and that Peter had gone off to Seven Gates to prepare for them, and then flopped down by the fire and thankfully took the cup of steaming cocoa that Charles passed him.

"That was good work, David. Downright sensible. We're packing up as fast as we can and the twins and young Percy here are dry and warm again. Mr Ringway's car won't start, so we can't do anything about that till tomorrow. We'll come back then to clear up this mess."

"But if it stops raining, which I doubt," Tom said, "then this camp is still all right. Don't let's give up yet. I don't suppose Mr Wilkins and Mr Ringway want to give up searching, anyway."

Mr Ringway beamed on the company while Mr Wilkins, in very decided tones, remarked, "Certainly not. I shall be back here tomorrow in the hope that the flood will have abated. But this is no place now for any of us, and as soon as this lad is warm and rested a little, I suggest we get back to the road."

"Good enough," Charles said. "And I hope you two gentlemen will honour us at Seven Gates tonight. Mr Ringway can telephone from there, and we can get a man from the garage on to his car tomorrow. Are we ready?"

It was a bedraggled and strange-looking procession that set out down the dingle ten minutes later, and when the party reached the clearing and the lights of the caravan glowed through the dark, Charles turned and called David.

"Car's not back, David. We'll go straight through to the road . . . Except Percy, of course. I can see his mother waiting for him."

There was an awkward pause, then Charles and Mr Ringway led the way into the wood and Mr Wilkins said, "Go to your mother, boy."

Tom, David and Jenny turned away from him when he snivelled, but Mary went up to him and said, "Maybe we're quits now, Percy."

Dickie flashed the light from his torch on to the boy's face, but all he said was, "Come on, twin. Let's go," and as the Lone Piners went off between the trees, the boy Percy stumbled and splashed blindly across to the caravan, knowing that never before in his spoiled and selfish life had he felt so miserable and lonely.

As the last stragglers reached the road they were almost blinded by the headlights of Smithson's great car and of another just behind.

"Good old Peter!" David said. "Here comes the taxi too," and when Smithson had pulled up he went across and said, "Thank you, sir. Your boy is safe back again and Mr Wilkins is staying with us. Good night!"

It must have been a long time since anyone had spoken to Mr Smithson like this, and he was so surprised that he merely nodded and turned the car into the wood.

The journey to Seven Gates was made in two relays—first Tom and the twins with Jenny, who got out at the post office, thinking it as well to tell her parents that she was safe and sound, and arranged for the driver to pick her up on his next journey when he brought David and the three men.

At Seven Gates all was orderly excitement. When the first party arrived, Peter, in a borrowed dressing-gown of her aunt's, was sitting in the great kitchen, toasting her toes by the roaring fire and sipping something hot from a glass. Her father and Uncle Micah, both smoking their pipes, were listening to her affectionately when Tom, the twins and Macbeth came in. But the twins were not allowed to stay long, for Mrs Sterling pounced on them and bustled them, protestingly, upstairs.

"No arguments and no nonsense, and it's no use appealing to Uncle Micah, Mary. Hot baths for you both and then hot drinks in a hot bed."

"Not *bed*!" Dickie wailed indignantly. "You can't put us to bed. It's not time yet, and we've only just got here—" and then his plaint was cut short by the slamming of a door and the gush of running water.

The rest of the party arrived half an hour later with a radiant Jenny looking particularly nice in a bright green dress.

"Hello, Peter darling. Hello, Tom, and good evening both Mr Sterlings," she began in her inimitable way. "I've told them at home that I shan't be home tonight. That was right, wasn't it? When we crossed the yard I saw a light in the barn, so I s'pose we are going back there, aren't we?"

"Uncle Micah lit the stove and the lamp for us, Jenny," Peter replied, "so we can all have supper there presently.

Hello, David. You look pretty wet and miserable. Next for the bath, you!"

An hour later all the Lone Piners, except the twins, were round their own stove, while the rain beat on the roof and filled again the huge puddles in the farmyard.

"The twins are livid with rage," Jenny was saying. "I went up to see them, but your Aunt Carol says she will lock them in if they get out of bed and try to come down . . . What are we going to do tomorrow?"

David yawned and stretched out his tired legs.

"The grown-ups are talking it over now," he said. "I s'pose that if it stops raining Mr Wilkins will want to go back to the dingle, and if he does we've promised to help him, but I'm sick of the sight of it."

"I'd like to explore that cave again and see if the waterfall is still there," Tom said. "I can hardly believe all that happened only a few hours ago. I'm dead tired now, anyway, so let's not worry about tomorrow until it happens. What about bed, David?"

"Are you coming up now, Peter?" Jenny asked.

"I nearly promised Aunt Carol I'd sleep indoors tonight, but I knew I couldn't really do that, so it wasn't a real promise," Peter replied.

And as they both snuggled into their sleeping-bags a few minutes later, the only sound was the relentless tattoo of rain on the roof and the rush of water in the gutters.

12. *Treasure Trove*

As the sun climbed up the eastern sky above the Stiper-stones the following morning and lit the old brown tiles on the roof of H.Q.2, Jenny, still in her sleeping-bag, stirred and began to dream.

She dreamed of something she had never seen in her short lifetime, and never could see either. At first she was lying in hot sunshine on the turf of a little hill overlooking a straight, white road which stretched away into the distance. Although she did not recognize the countryside, the outline of a whale-backed hill with some irregular piles of rocks on the summit in the distance seemed vaguely familiar. Then she saw a cloud of dust far down the road, and soon the cloud was stabbed with shafts of light, as if the sun was glinting on bright metal.

And so it was, for as she watched, spellbound on her little hill, a company of soldiers in unfamiliar uniform came marching towards her. They sang as they came swinging along with great strides—a song the words of which Jenny could not recognize. Each soldier carried a gleaming shield and a long spear, and wore plated armour which shone like bronze and a kilt which looked as if it might be made of metal strips. Their brown legs were bare except for shin-guards and sandals. And on the proud head of each was a great helmet, with a heavy chinpiece and a scarlet comb of stiff horsehair that flickered in the wind. Then, rather like the television, this picture faded into another, which was harder to understand. It was dusk now, in a valley overshadowed by gaunt hills, and some sort of low house was blazing fiercely. Men and women, dressed in a style which Jenny did not recognize, were running round the burning building, and some had bundles in their arms. The picture changed again to a kicking baby in a woman's arms, and somehow in this picture her own strange silver spoon kept intruding. And with this vision still in her mind she woke and found herself clutching her spoon, which she was still wearing round her neck.

Peter was still sleeping quietly beside her and did not even stir as Jenny slipped out of her sleeping-bag and dressed. Very carefully and quietly she crept down the ladder into the great barn. David was still asleep in his cubicle, as was Tom in his bedroom next door. Jenny bent over Tom closely and squeezed the lobe of his ear between her finger and thumb and whispered, "Wake up, Tom . . . Quietly . . . Please wake quickly, Tom!" He stirred, rolled over and tried to sit up as he recognized her. She put a finger to her lips.

"*Please*, Tom," she breathed, "don't wake David, but do please dress and come outside. I want you. I've got an idea."

He was with her in three minutes, but still looked sleepy, tousled and bewildered.

"What's wrong now, Jen? And why all this hush business?"

"Tom! Isn't it a gorgeous morning?"

"Maybe it is, but why get me up to show me?"

Jenny kicked a stone idly into a puddle and then looked up at him under her lashes.

"Will you come with me now, Tom, back to Greystone Dingle, and see what it looks like after the flood?"

"But why? Why now, before breakfast? And why not the others?"

"Don't ask such stupid questions, Tom. I just want to go and I thought it would be fun if we went together . . . After all," she added, almost without realizing it, "you did give me the spoon."

He looked at her quietly for a moment and then smiled and nodded.

"All right. Thanks for asking me. I'll just leave a note for David telling them not to wait breakfast. How do we go?"

"On bikes. I'll borrow Dad's for you. Hurry up!"

Tom went back into the barn, scribbled on a page of David's notebook, tore it out and put it on the top of the stove, which was now cold.

Jenny was waiting by the white gate leading down through the whispering trees, but she did not say much as they slithered through the mud down to the road, except, "I've had a most peculiar dream, Tom."

"Is that why I've got to rush about like this on an empty stomach?" he protested.

"This dream *was* peculiar, Tom. It was about Roman soldiers and a house burning, and when I woke up I was clutching your spoon."

Tom was about to ask, "What's that got to do with it?" when he had enough sense to say nothing. Maybe all would be made clear to him before long!

It was a perfect morning, with a rain-washed sky, when they reached Barton village post office.

"Better come into the yard with me, Tom. I'm sure Dad won't mind if you borrow his bike."

Tom was not so sure, but Jenny was so insistent about going to the dingle that he shrugged his shoulders and helped her out with the bicycles. Mr Harman did not often ride his bicycle, and its appearance suggested that he was not very interested in it either. Tom looked at it with distaste.

"Don't be difficult, Tom," Jenny said brightly. "It's perfectly all right if you're sensible. There's a pump for the tyres in the corner of the shed . . . I think you have to be careful of the chain because that jams sometimes—at least it did once and Dad fell off."

Tom did his best, but as Mr Harman was taller than he was and as he could not find a spanner, the saddle was of little use to him. But at last they saw the mountain on their right, with the pinewood below, and Tom knew that his period of torture was over for the time being.

"I'm not cycling any longer, Jen," he said as he dropped the hated bicycle on the grass verge. "What do we do now?"

Jenny jumped off too, and laughed.

"You are funny when you're cross, Tom. It was better and quicker to bike than to walk, and I think this is fun. I like coming out like this without the others for once, and I want to see what the water has done to the valley."

It was difficult to resist her high spirits, so Tom laughed good-naturedly as she dropped her bicycle beside the other and turned towards the track through the wood, which was more like the bed of a river this morning. They noticed that water was still running across the road which was covered with mud, stones, pine needles and debris. Then they splashed up the sticky path until they reached the clearing and saw the Smithsons' caravan, but not their car.

"Looks deserted," Tom said, and walked up boldly and tapped on the window. The door with the broken lock was fastened now with a piece of rope on the outside, so as it was obvious that Tom's guess was correct they went on up the valley.

"What are you looking for, Jen?" he asked. "Do you want to go as far as the cave?"

"I don't know, Tom. Honestly I don't, although I would like to see whether the beginning of this stream is still in the same place. There's still a lot of water in it."

The stream was still four or five times bigger than when they had first seen it, and yesterday's flood had brought down a lot of mud and rubbish. But everything looked different in this morning's bright sunshine, and Jenny was singing cheerfully as she swung along the narrow track a yard or so in front of Tom. She was still leading when they came to the rock beyond which Mr Smithson had been scraping among the stones when they had first come up to the cave. As soon as she was past the rock she stopped short and Tom barged into her.

"Something has happened here, Tom," she said. "It's

different. The ground has been washed away and the water is running over something bright."

She ran forward excitedly and went down on her knees in the mud.

"My dream, Tom! This isn't it really, but it's something to do with it, I know . . . It must be, Tom, because I wanted to come here so badly ever since I woke up . . . What is this, Tom? It looks like part of a floor all made up of little bits of coloured stone. I s'pose the river was stopped a bit by the rock here and the water has washed the soil away."

Tom flopped down beside her. He was puzzled, but excited, too, as he said: "Somehow or other I reckon your old Mr Wilkins ought to see this. Would you like to go back for him while I stay on guard here?"

But Jenny was looking at a heap of mud and rubbish piled up against a rock on the other side of the stream.

"There's something sticking out of that mud, Tom. What is it?"

Together they splashed through the stream and plunged eager hands into the mess of mud, and found what was to be known later as the Greystone Treasure—six pieces of wonderful silver plate which was once used at the table of a wealthy Roman sixteen centuries ago. To Tom and Jenny the three plates, two goblets and beautifully shaped bowl did not look like treasure, for they were black and so dirty that it was not possible to see the engraved designs on each. But Jenny was sure.

"This is it, Tom! This is the Roman treasure Mr Wilkins believed was here. I'm sure it is. And that bit of stone floor is part of a Roman's house . . . And we've found it, Tom. You bought me the spoon that began all this adventure, and now we've finished it together."

Tom fingered one of the beautifully shaped goblets, with its fluted stem and big round base, and then smiled at her.

"People must be crackers if they think all this old junk is

worth a lot of money, but I'm glad it's you that found it, Jen . . . Let's take it back to show the old man, and meanwhile we'd better cover up the Roman floor with mud. If anyone else comes this way they might be curious . . . Or would you like to take the treasure back while I stay on guard here?"

"No, Tom. I won't move a step without you. This is yours as much as mine, and we'll take it back together and surprise them all . . . I believe I remember an old sack in the cave. Will you go up and get that and I'll stay here to gloat!"

About fifteen minutes later they were back where they had left the bicycles, and although most of the road was uphill back to Barton Beach, even Tom was too excited now to worry much about the discomfort of riding all the way on the pedals. They left the bicycles in the yard behind the post office again and, after what seemed an eternity, they came to the last white gate and looked across the farmyard of Seven Gates.

"Here you are, Jenny," Tom said as he offered her the sack. "Take your million pounds. You found it. Let's go in and surprise them."

The doors of H.Q.2 were wide open and there was the clatter of many voices as they walked across the farmyard. Then they saw that breakfast was not yet over and that Mr Wilkins, Mr Ringway, the two Mr Sterlings and Aunt Carol were there as guests.

For a moment Tom and Jenny stood in the doorway, and then Mary saw them and gave a whoop of welcome.

"Where have you been, you two? What have you been doing?"

Everyone stopped talking and turned to look at the two adventurers, and this was Jenny's really great moment. She smiled at them all, walked to the long trestle table, and stopped beside Mr Wilkins.

The old man turned in surprise.

"Good morning, my dear. And where have you been, so

early in the morning after yesterday's exhausting adventures?"

Jenny leaned over him and pushed his plate and cup to one side. Then she kissed the top of his head, emptied the sack on to the table-cloth and said, "I told you the Lone Piners would help you, Mr Wilkins. I think this is what you've been looking for."

Pandemonium followed this dramatic moment, and it was some time before Tom and Jenny were able to tell their story coherently. Mr Ringway was almost beside himself with excitement, and when he heard about the portion of Roman pavement he grabbed Mr Wilkins by the arm and made for the door.

"Greystone must not be left unguarded for one instant," he said. "Come, Wilkins! Come at once! This is history."

Then he ran back into the barn and shook hands with Jenny and Tom.

"What about us?" Dickie said. "We did a lot too, Mr Ringway."

"If you've got time," Mary added, "we'll show you an underground lake that we fell in. Maybe that place is full of old things too."

While they were speaking a familiar car crawled through the mud into the farmyard, and with a rapturous cry of "Daddy!" Mary dashed through the puddles with Macbeth at her heels.

When Mr Morton was able to disentangle himself and the greetings and introductions were over, he explained that it was too wet for further camping and that he had come to take them home.

"But we've found a million pounds," Mary said. "Or Jenny has, which is nearly the same thing, because—"

"I know, Mary! I quite understand," Mr Morton smiled. "It's the same thing because you have a secret understanding . . . Now before someone tells me the full story, I've brought a telegram addressed to David. We thought we had better open it, David, just in case we had to reply," and he put his hand in his pocket and handed his elder son an envelope.

Everyone stopped talking, as people always do when a telegram arrives, and David moved a few steps away. Peter was at his elbow and Tom and Jenny just behind him as he unfolded the thin paper and read the message. Then he looked up at his friends and laughed.

"It's from Rye. Listen, chaps. '*We may want Lone Piners soon have just seen Ballinger again up to no good we wouldn't be surprised Jon and Penny.*'"

The story you have just finished is one of the adventures of the members of the Lone Pine Club. Each adventure is complete in itself and there are now nineteen of them. The complete list is as follows:

The author hopes that you have enjoyed this story and would like to know what you think of it. You can write to him, and he will answer your letter, which should be addressed to:

Malcolm Saville,
c/o Armada Books,
14 St. James's Place,
London, SW1A 1PF.